LOST AND FOUND

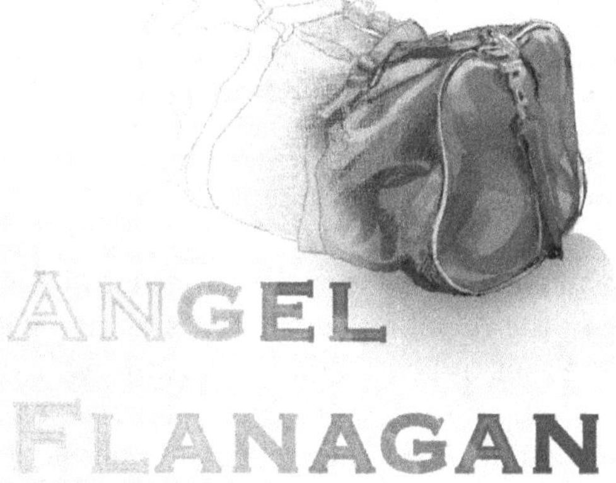

ANGEL FLANAGAN

Cover image: Rebekah Wetmore
Editor: Andrew Wetmore

ISBN: 978-1-990187-05-6
First edition July, 2021

2475 Perotte Road, Perotte
Annapolis County, NS B0S 1A0
moosehousepress.com
info@moosehousepress.com

We live and work in Mi'kma'ki, the ancestral and unceded territory of the Mi'kmaq People. This territory is covered by the "Treaties of Peace and Friendship" which Mi'kmaq and Wolastoqiyik (Maliseet) People first signed with the British Crown in 1725. The treaties did not deal with surrender of lands and resources but in fact recognized Mi'kmaq and Wolastoqiyik (Maliseet) title and established the rules for what was to be an ongoing relationship between nations. We are all Treaty people.

For Jamie, Dorian and Dylan.
They are the reason I do everything.

This is a work of fiction.
The author has created the characters, conversations, interactions, and events; and any resemblance of any character to any real person is coincidental.

Contents

Angel Flanagan

1: Party time

It was elbow to elbow at the bar, but that didn't stop Adam from noticing Denise at work. Soon as he arrived, his crazy bitch radar started going off. The round stage in the middle of the club lit up like a beacon. Denise was a siren screaming out into the night. Shit, the last girl Adam needed Sam to see tonight. He was trying to cheer him up, not make him more depressed.

Adam brought Sam to the bar, so they had their backs to the stage. He had hoped Denise would be off tonight. Oh well, fuck it, they'd have to have a few drinks and ignore her. Soon a new dancer would start shaking her tits.

They weren't planning on staying long. A short pit stop. Shit to do later, but Adam found it hard to see Sam so upset. Hell, tits and a few refreshments should pick up his spirits. How could he be so down? He'd only been with that chick for a few months.

Adam even had a bit of coke for after they left the club. From Thomas, along with a little cash, a treat to have after they did the delivery. He patted the old gym bag he had hooked over the back of Sam's chair. Wouldn't want to lose track of it.

He looked around. Thomas wasn't here yet. Too early. Thomas came to work after midnight most nights. It rarely got rowdy before then. His hulking presence in the corner kept people in line. No one wanted to mess with Thomas. A pile of muscles with no neck. A big square head sticking out of his shoulders like some mad scientist left out a piece of the monster.

Adam knew Trisha would be here tonight. Behind the bar as usual. She wasn't a dancer, although beautiful enough.

Trisha waved in his direction and hollered over the music, "Hey there, handsome stranger, what can I get you?"

He almost didn't hear her; more like he read her lips. Adam loved her lips. He could look at her all day. In a strip club, full of beautiful young women of all shapes and sizes, he only had eyes for Trisha.

He yelled back, "The usual, Trisha my darlin': two double whiskys, on the rocks."

Then he leaned in quick and kissed her. He took his time, which earned them a few catcalls and cheers from the people around them, but he paid them no mind. He wanted to do more than just kiss her. He couldn't wait for her to get off work. Adam loved his Trisha: she made him happy. He didn't care about her job or her age. Trisha was an amazing person, beautiful to boot. She never judged people and helped anyone she could. She had no kids of her own, but she was like a Mom to most of the girls here, and the guys, too. Everyone needed someone to care about them.

That's why she still worked here after all this time. Usually, people didn't stay working at the club for long. They moved on fast. For some, it wasn't the dream job they expected. The money was usually good, but sometimes what came with it was too much.

It was a little different for feature dancers. They got to travel, their acts got promoted, and they had photos to sign and sell. Feature girls made a lot more money than regular girls. Still, one day, they all wanted out to do other things.

That's where Trisha came in. She never pushed anyone to do anything, but if you wanted a change and needed some help, she was there for you.

A new song with a lot of low bass started shaking the big sub-woofers all around him. Adam turned around. He was in luck. This time the woman outlined by the spotlight on the main stage wasn't Denise. A tall brunette with short hair and small tits. Not the biggest in the place, but they looked real and were still a nice little handful. She played shy as she took off her long, black gloves, one finger at a time. Her legs made up for the small boobs. Wrapped in thigh high shiny black leather boots with stiletto heels. Not much else to her outfit: A little fishnet and see-through black fabric here and there.

He clinked glasses with Sam and drank his off in one drink. "Come on, Sam, cheer up. Things will work out. Until then, look around you. This is a happy place. As long as you like boobs...You like boobs, don't ya?"

"Yeah, I like tits fine."

"Well, then, feast your eyes upon the stage."

"It only makes me miss Jane. I can't help it, I love her. She's the best thing that ever happened to me. I wish I could stop thinking about her."

"I'm sorry, man. You guys can work things out. Give her a little time."

"I'm afraid it's already too late. Jane doesn't want to be with me anymore."

"Jane loves you. She wants you to grow up and lay off the drugs a little. Trisha wants me to do the same."

"I know, and I should have listened to her. The last two weeks felt like two years without her. Trisha didn't leave you even though she wants you to change. She's still with you. Jane left. It's my fault I'm on my own."

Adam had no answer that would make any difference. So he said nothing and ordered another round for Sam and himself.

When he turned back around, there was a pretty, young, almost-naked woman at Sam's elbow. Funny how that always seemed to happen in places like this. Girls that hot didn't show up and start talking to guys like them in the real world. This place brought many things to mind, but real wasn't one of them. There was a lot of dyed hair, heavy makeup, and over-sized, doctor-assisted breasts.

Adam thought the rack on the chick chatting up Sam looked pretty real. This was perfect: a new girl, and she seemed to like Sam. Liked him at least as much as any stripper likes her customers.

Adam stuffed a couple of bills under one of the many leather straps the girl wore. It was the bones of a dress. The black leather looked great against her skin. "Take my buddy out back and show him a real good time, would ya, honey?"

"That would be my pleasure." She smiled and took Sam by the hand and tried to lead him away. He resisted. She looked at Adam. "I can't force him, hon."

"Come on, Sammy, go have fun for a little while. Later on, after I drop off the package, we can get fucked up and forget all our problems. If you're lucky, we can get this little lady to join me, you and Trisha after this place closes. What's your name, sweet cheeks?"

"Sara."

"Is that your real name or your stage name?" He didn't care, just making small talk. What else do you talk about with a dancer?

"My real name, sweetheart, I only have one name. Ain't got no time for fake shit."

"Nice to meet you, Sara. This is Sam. You know Trisha, the bartender? She's my girl. How about the four of us meet up after closing and have some fun. Sam needs some fun. Everyone does. We have to go see a friend first. Won't take long."

"Might be a fun little adventure," Sara said. "I'll talk to Trish. In the meantime, how about another round on me?"

"How about that, Sam? This lady wants to buy you a drink. What do you say?"

"I say, thank you, Sara, and bottoms up," Sam said.

The rest of the night passed them by in a blur of breasts, booze, and music. Adam got up more than once to go deliver the stuff, but it wasn't time yet. He was willing to leave Sam at the club. He thought about doing the drop himself.

By the time it was time to go do it, the three of them had gotten so drunk they could hardly walk.

That girl Sara stayed stuck to Sam like glue. Since she was kinda hanging out with them, she wasn't making any money. None left to tip her with either. The drinks and the money for the lap dance had tapped him out. She didn't know that yet, though, and he wasn't going to tell her. Sam was having fun, and that was what Adam had been trying to make happen by coming here.

2: Dirty dancing

Sara was waiting for Denise to finish her last set when Sam and Adam walked into the club. Sam looked like his dog died. She wondered what was up with him, although Sara didn't mind seeing him look sad. She didn't know Sam at all, or Adam for that matter. All she knew was that he was Denise's ex-boyfriend and Mikey's Dad. His deadbeat Dad. Seeing him at the club would piss Denise off.

Sara hurried backstage hoping to keep Denise from losing her mind and flipping right out. She pushed the beaded curtain out of the way and watched as Denise wiped the sweat off her face and neck with a fuzzy towel.

"Hey, babe, you look more than great out there, as usual. You should be a movie star, and I don't mean porn." She took a breath, then jumped to the point. "Sam and his buddy are at the bar, talking to Trisha."

"Yeah, I saw him when I got off the stage. All I needed to make my night complete. His so-called best friend Adam is Trisha's boyfriend. So it sucks they have an excuse and balls to come in here when I'm working. He knows it gets to me, too, or else he would stay as far away as possible."

Denise buried her face in the towel again and screamed into it. Sara didn't understand everything she said, but she caught a couple of words, like 'asshole' and 'fuck'.

Sara tried to put her arms around her, but Denise

stiffened a little and pushed her away. She was too strong to accept a hug now. If she did take the hug she might cry and lose the anger. She didn't want to let it go.

"Not here, someone will see us. It's okay, I'm alright, I'm okay. I'm not going to go overboard," Denise said, with a sad, bitter smile. "That ass doesn't have any money for Mike, but he's got money for tits."

Sara could tell by the way her eyes were starting to bulge out of her head that Denise was right on the edge. She hoped she could calm her down enough to avoid a brawl. Thanks to the gods of strip clubs and exes that Denise wasn't drinking tonight. Shit would have already hit the fan.

"I called him asking for some money for diapers two days ago, and he blew me off, said he was broke. That he would buy diapers when Mikey lived with him. I wanted to kick him in the teeth. I hung up. It was useless to fight with him. That's what he wants me to do, fight with him, make myself look like a fool. How the fuck could I have ever loved him?"

"Come and have a smoke with me. We can talk about it outside."

The two of them made their way through the back rooms and darkened halls to a fire door. They stuck a chair in it and went out for a smoke in the alley.

Sara took Denise's shaking hand in both of hers. "We all make mistakes, hon. People change, things change. You gotta let this go. Take him to court and get a judge to order him to pay child support. Let a lawyer deal with everything, so you don't have to even see him. It would be easier on you and Mikey."

Then a thought struck her. "I have an idea. How about I go over there, flirt a bit and get him so drunk he "loses" whatever money he has? If one of the other girls gets their tits out first, they'll get his money. He doesn't know anything about us yet, does he?"

"No, but I don't want to pull you into this shit."

"I'm with you babe, I'm already in." Sara flashed an impish smile. "He won't know what hit him."

Sara kissed Denise on the forehead, a quick peck. Another peck on the tip of her nose. On her lips she lingered longer, savouring the taste of her mouth. "I'll fix everything."

Back inside, Sara took a look in a mirror—there were plenty of them all over the club. She was finished dancing for the night anyway. She had done her time on stage early on, when the bar was half empty.

Now she was mingling with the crowd. The ones who hadn't spent all their money yet. Sara had planned on doing a private dance or two. She wasn't wearing much of anything. It looked like the designer had run out of fabric, and used scraps to make the dress. Black leather straps crisscrossed all over her body, from her throat to her ankles. Covering some things, while leaving others completely bare. Free advertising: looking was free. If they wanted to touch, they had to pay. She might sell her body, but she wasn't cheap. There was only one reason she did any of this. The money. The admiration of drooling drunks, men or women, wasn't near enough.

3: Nosy

"You guys want another round?" Trisha asked.

"Yes, please!" Sara answered.

"I gotta take a leak," Adam said.

"Me too, be right back, cutie." Sam gave Sara's left butt cheek a squeeze as he headed in the general direction of the bathroom.

Sara knocked the bag off the back of Sam's chair to the floor and unzipped the top a little to check for money. She was surprised to find what looked like heroin under an old t-shirt instead.

She closed the bag and hung it back on the chair just as Trisha returned to the table with their drinks. "Can't wait 'til you get off work and can have a drink with us," Sara smiled at Trisha.

"I'll be done soon, Max said he will close up for me, so we can get out of here earlier. We can have a private party at my place."

"That sounds great! Max is awesome! It's a date."

She watched the boys returning to the table, they weren't staggering much yet; she better keep pushing drinks on them. Sara wasn't going to just steal his money: she was going to steal his whole bag, see how he deals with that. Asshole should have bought the diapers.

"Drink up, boys, this round is on me," she laughed.

"Next one is on me, then we're leaving this place for more private fun!" Trisha said. She winked at Adam and turned back to the bar.

4: Jane

"So what is the plan?" Jim asked.

"A light rap on the door should be enough to get her attention," Bob said. "Keep quiet and follow my lead." He pointed to the other side of the doorway. "When she opens the door for me, we will both push in before she can close it again. I'll grab her, you stick her with this." Bob passed a small syringe full of clear liquid to Jim. "She will be out like a light, then we get her to the car. If anyone asks, we'll say my girlfriend has the flu, and we are driving her to her Mom's to a cozy blanket and some nice warm soup."

"I can handle it, Bobby boy. You don't need to babysit me. You are the one who is still wet behind the ears."

"Be sure you don't fucking stick me with that shit, okay? I'll be a lot harder to carry around. I'm not as pretty as her, and I won't like the headache that follows sleepy time."

No answer on the first knock. The second time he tried a little harder. He heard a small noise on the other side of the door. A quiet rustle of clothes and the sound of the safety chain rattling.

"Wait a sec," a sleepy feminine voice came through the door.

It seemed to take longer than winter in February for her to open the door. On the bright side, half asleep meant off guard. Perfect. Things were going his way.

People were so trusting around here. Shitty small town. Small to him anyways. He was a little surprised that the safety chain was even engaged. Most people didn't even lock their doors around here.

Jane opened the door. Her eyes weren't open all the way. She looked like shit. He had thought she was going to be a hottie. Looked like he was wrong. She didn't look like a morning person and needed a bit of makeup to suit his taste. He liked girls who took care of themselves, who took a little pride in their appearance. His last girlfriend would not even go out to the mailbox without a full face of makeup and hair on point.

He doubted she even looked out the peephole before she opened the door. It wouldn't have mattered if she did. He was ready to talk his way inside if he had to. At first glance, Bob seemed completely innocent. He looked like an inconspicuous door-to-door salesman. Suit, tie and a briefcase. He was young and good-looking, his quick smile opened lots of doors, and legs for him. If Jim had knocked on the door she might have hesitated a little, or not.

Jane was still rubbing the sleep out of her eyes when they slipped in the door fast as water over a rock. Bob grabbed her and Jim stuck her with the needle. It couldn't have gone any smoother.

They loaded her in the backseat of the car and were on their merry way. By the look of the flyers piled up in front of the door to the other apartment in the building, no one was living there. No neighbours, everything was going his way.

"Sleeping beauty isn't going to wake up for a few hours. We have plenty of time to get her to the hideout and set up the meet," Bob said.

"I'll call the boss and let him know where we're at."

"Good. Tell him no one was around and it went off without a hitch. Might make him not so pissed off."

"Pissed off is an understatement," Jim said. "At least it wasn't our fuck up."

"He knows he screwed up the deal, he chose the delivery guys. He's more mad at himself than us."

"I'd like to get a few minutes alone with blondie here, if ya know what I mean." Jim snickered with an evil sparkle in his eye.

"You keep your dirty little hands off her until the boss tells you different. I don't want him mad at me for not keeping you under control."

"You don't run me, rookie. You'd do best to remember that."

"All I do is what Thomas tells me to do. So you can back the fuck off."

"We'll see," Jim said. "Do we have to go get Trisha, too? She won't be as easy to grab."

"No, Tom said to let her be for now, but make sure we have someone to watch her like a hawk."

"If they try to contact her or show up at the club, we will know. She could be a good source of info. We can always find her if we need to. She only ever goes to the club and her place."

Bob nodded. "They will give up the shit to save that little cutie."

"And once they do?"

"Easy, Jimmy, you know what to do. Should be easy as pie to make it look like what it is, a drug deal gone bad. You do your part to shut everyone up. We make sure there are no witnesses or evidence. I can take care of evidence with some cleansing fire. The cops will write it off as a bunch of dead junkie criminals. They won't even look that hard. Lew spends big bucks to make sure of that."

Bob was happy his little plan had worked, way better than Jim's maniac plan. Jim was like a bull moose. Big, loud and clumsy. A blind and deaf person would have noticed two men dragging around a screaming woman in the trunk of their car. Bob was a little smoother. That was why Thomas had put him in charge of this pickup.

5: Rainbow Motel

Listening to the falling rain had always been one of Lynda's favourite things to do. Especially at night. The only thing she enjoyed more was walking silent, unseen through the wet darkness. Most of the time, no one even noticed her standing still in the shadows. Everyone else was always in a great big hurry when it rained. Lynda was the opposite. She took her time. Usually it calmed her, but tonight even the dancing rain couldn't lighten her mood.

As the liquid trickled its way down the windowpane, it seemed to call to her like something lost. A fragment of a memory dragged at her thoughts. As she tried to grasp it, it slipped away into the past. Like the silvery grey fog that had drifted in with the warm summer storm. She let it drift away. Whatever the memory was, she didn't want it.

The buzzing of her cell phone brought her attention back to the hotel room. It was cozy and dry, although a little worn around the edges with threadbare rugs and faded curtains.

She grabbed at the phone as a text saying "I'm on my way" flashed across the screen.

Finally. A small smile came to her lips for the first time in what seemed like weeks. She lit a cigarette, looked back out at the rain and settled down to wait for the fun to begin.

Noise woke her from a light sleep and a dream about Jane. She tried to remember it before it faded. It wasn't a dream. It was a memory of when Jane was about nine years old. Lynda had taken her to the beach; they had fun splashing in the water and playing in the sand. It was a good afternoon. It was the first time Jane, or Lynda herself, had even smiled since the night their parents had died.

All her memories were good and bad tied together. It was always there, in the background of their lives. There was always that sense of something missing. There were no good childhood memories. Every happy event ended in a fight, thus becoming a bad memory. Smiling Jane on a beach was a rare good memory.

Lynda looked outside. It was almost daylight. How long had she been waiting? Where the hell was Sam?

She should have known it wasn't going to be simple. Dealing with Sam as of late was usually difficult. Like skinning an eel. Slippery, slimy, dirty work. With any luck, you wind up with a little something that makes it worth it in the end. One thing she had learned so far was sometimes you had to take whatever help you could get. Until she got the whole story out of Sam she would have to try to keep her cool.

She checked her phone: no missed calls or texts. Nothing except the first one. It was short but got the point across: "It's Sam, I have to talk to you about Jane. It's important. Meet me at the Rainbow Motel tonight. Please."

That had only been this morning. Lynda thought it was strange how time could seem to be passing so slow and still so fast. Like a broken watch the second hand seems to slow down, stick, then jump ahead without warning. The hands of the watch might break, but for some reason, the gears of time never turn backward.

Now she was even more worried. It had been too long, something was up. The headache was back. She didn't think it ever left anymore. Pain radiated from her right eye socket, making thoughts a distant signal dimmed by heavy fog. What if Sam wasn't coming? What next? She thought about that while digging in her purse for something to dull the throbbing pain.

Another noise startled her, this time much louder. Lynda got up and pulled back the curtain. There was an old car smoking and sputtering. It backfired a couple of times when they tried to shut it off. They parked pretty much on top of the old flower bed filled with weeds in front of the building.

The rusty passenger door squeaked open and out jumped, well, staggered Adam. Great, all she needed, someone else to babysit. Shouldn't have surprised her, Sam never went too far without his new sidekick. Lynda didn't know him very well, but he'd been around town for a few months now. Lynda had gotten the feeling that Jane didn't like him very much, either.

She opened the hotel room door wide. "About time you assholes got here! What the fuck is up with that piece of shit car?"

Sam looked at her sheepishly. "Sorry, Lynda, that's why it took so long to get here. Mine's in the shop, so I had to call Adam. I was lucky to get a ride over here at all."

Lynda looked at Sam, the car, and Adam, not sure who she should yell at first. The car was damn near a model T. She rubbed her temple. She supposed she should be glad they even showed up. She pointed into the room. "You've wasted more than enough time already. Get in here and explain to me where is Jane and what the hell is going on. I've been texting and calling her since I got your message. No answer from Jane."

She pushed them both through the narrow doorway and slammed the door closed. Lynda might be small but she was mighty. "Jane always has her phone. Always. She always answers my messages. Always. You'd better talk fuckin' fast, or in about five seconds I am calling the police to report my sister missing!"

"No!" Sam yelled, "No cops. Listen to me and I'll explain everything."

He reached for her arm. She pulled away, not because it was Sam, it was her regular reaction when anyone touched her. She hated it when people touched her.

When he spoke, his voice was quiet, she almost didn't hear him. "Everything is completely out of control and I don't know how to stop it. I know I fucked up, but please listen. Okay? Then you can yell at me all you want. Hell, maybe I'll even yell at myself."

6: Good intentions

Lynda's dark eyes were snapping and ringed with black from lack of sleep, and her brown hair was a dark tangled mess. Sam thought, not for the first time, that she and Jane didn't look like sisters at all. From the old photos he'd seen and the few stories he'd heard, Jane had their blonde mother's looks and mild temperament. Lynda resembled their dark-haired, impulsive father.

Sam tried to think of the best way to explain everything. He had been trying to figure out how to tell her since he first found out Jane was gone. He hardly knew what had happened himself. It was all lost in a weekend-long burn that had seemed like it took only minutes. He took a deep breath and blurted out, "They took Jane and it's all my fault!"

"What? Why would anyone take Jane?" Lynda crossed the room and grabbed Sam by his jacket. "Where is my sister?"

"Lewis has her. We don't know where."

"Who is Lewis and why is Jane with him? Talk fast, Sam."

"Alright," he said. "Short story is, Adam and me were trying to move some stuff for a guy named Thomas to make some quick money."

"We got drunk and high at the club and someone ripped us off," Adam said. He was almost hiding in the corner. "There is no point beating around the bush. Tell her everything, Sam. She needs to know the truth."

"I'm trying to tell her. Shut up, will ya? It's my turn. Let me talk." Sam turned back to Lynda. "Thomas has a boss in the Valley, his name is Lewis. We've never met him. I've heard he's a real serious fella. He wants his money or his product. He wants it back yesterday, scratch that, he wants it back last week."

He rubbed his hands across his scruffy face. "That's why they took Jane. We have to find the gym bag and give it back before it's too late. He looked at her with blood-shot eyes.

"What do you mean 'too late'? Jane is missing, it is already too late! What fucking 'stuff' were you trying to deliver? I can not believe you two pulled my sister and me into this mess," Lynda said. "I'm calling the cops."

"No, that will only make it worse," Adam said. "No cops or else they'll kill her. It's not an idle threat, they mean it." He was quiet as usual, but his voice carried. Sam crossed the carpet in a sudden burst of nervous energy and pushed Adam against the dresser. They scuffled for a minute, sending the lamp crashing to the floor. They pushed and shoved each other until they tripped and landed among the broken glass.

"This entire mess is your fault, Adam," Sam said, finally pushing him away. "I should never have listened to you."

Sam leaned back on the wall behind him and slid halfway down it, like a collapsing hot air balloon. "'It'll be easy,' you said. You said, 'No one will even know it happened. You will finally have enough money to get a real house for your woman. Instead of shitty one-room apartments with no hot water and doors that don't even lock. All we have to do is deliver a package, easy money, man.' So easy, so fuckin' easy..." Sam trailed off and sank the rest of the way to the dirty green shag carpet.

Adam stumbled a few steps away and fell over his own feet. "You think I wanted this to happen? Screw you, man. I was only trying to help you guys out."

"You're a regular fuckin' cub scout, aren't ya?" Sam said. "Every time I listen to you my life turns to shit. You were trying to help you like you always do. It had nothing to do with helping us."

"Don't be so fuckin' paranoid, man. I love you guys. I was so thinking of you—you need the money pretty bad."

"Stop it, you two!" Lynda said. "Fighting with each other isn't going to help! Pick your dumb asses up off the floor. Now, tell me, what we are going to do to get my sister back? When did you last see the bag? What club were you partying at?"

Sam said, "We were at that strip club, Hidden Pleasures. Adam's girlfriend works there. She's a bartender. Like you."

"If she works at Pleasures, I can tell you without a doubt, she is nothing at all like me."

Sam hoped that Adam let that comment slide. They didn't need to argue whether there was anything wrong with working at a strip club. A job was a job and work was work. People had to eat and put a roof over their heads. Lynda was already mad enough. Another stupid fight was the last thing they all needed right now.

"We stopped in to say hi and have one drink. Somehow we ended up there for a little longer than we planned. We went home with Trisha and a new girl. We partied for a while and I passed out. Next thing I know I'm getting a phone call from a strange number, asking where we were and where the package was. We should have delivered it already. At first, I was so wasted I didn't even know what package the guy meant. To top it off we kinda got lost on the way here."

"New girl from the club, what the fuck?" Lynda said. "Why wasn't Jane with you? Lost on the way here? How can you get lost on the way to save Jane? Whatever you are doing needs to stop. You two need to straighten up."

"Well, me and Janie haven't been getting along for the past few weeks," Sam said. "She's been staying at her friend Tara's house the last two weeks"

"This is all news to me. Jane didn't tell me anything was wrong. I didn't know you were having trouble. I didn't know she moved out. Why didn't she tell me she needed a place to stay?" Lynda said. "A couple of weeks? And you are out looking for skin already? It sounds like you have a broken heart."

"Sounds like you don't know a lot of things about Jane. She may be your little sister, but she's all grown up. Whatever, it doesn't matter now," Sam said. "We have to be careful, whoever grabbed Jane is watching us right now. I don't want anybody else to get hurt."

"We should call the police," Lynda said. "This is way over our heads. We need help."

"Oh yeah, call the cops and tell them what? Someone stole our heroin and now my girlfriend is being held hostage?" Sam snorted. "I'm sure they will be right over to help us."

"Fine, have it your way, no cops. For now. I guess our first stop is the club. Adam, you have to talk to Trisha. Do you think she could have taken it?"

"No way, a hundred percent sure she wouldn't steal from me!"

"You'd bet your life on it? That's what you are doing, betting my baby sister's life that your girlfriend didn't try to fuck you over. If we go to her for help and she's the one who took the bag, we're screwed."

"Fuck, yeah, I'm sure it wasn't her. She is not the

sneaky type," Adam said. "She is as honest as can be, doesn't hide her feelings. If she was going to take it, she'd take it right in front of me. She's gonna kill me when she finds out about all this. Trish hates that shit, and it takes a lot to piss her off. She's been after me to clean up for ages. I keep half-assing it. I hope this isn't the last straw."

"I like this Trisha more and more," Lynda said. "Do you think she could at least find out if any strangers were around that night? Or any regulars acting strange? The bouncers or bartenders should have noticed something. We need that bag. It's the key to saving Jane."

Adam said, "We can't go anywhere near the club. We'll have to go talk to Trish at her place. That will be iffy enough. If anyone at the club saw anything, she will be able to find out all the details by tonight."

7: Munchies

Lynda left the hotel and stopped at the first convenience store she came to. Was an Irving gas station and Tim Horton's. The coffee smelled like heaven. She needed to eat. She wasn't a big eater and when things got crazy she ate even less. She was going to pass out if she didn't eat something.

Lynnie walked into the gas station, grabbed a chocolate bar, a Pepsi and plain chips. That should keep her alive. She brought it all up to the counter. The pretty, long-haired girl behind the counter had a name tag that said "Mandy". She didn't look much older than Jane. She looked bored and happy to have a customer to chat with. "Awesome snack choices. Glad to see you are hitting all the important food groups, caffeine, chocolate, salty and crunchy. I love this stuff."

"Me too. I'm not much of a cook. Takes too much patience."

On impulse she grabbed a bag of whoppers, her sister's favourite chocolate treat, and added it to her pile. "I hate these, not enough chocolate. The cookie part is a damn lie, pretending to be a nice chocolate ball, but for some reason my little sister loves them. I think I'll get her some."

"That's sweet of you. You are a great big sister! Wish I had a sister that brought me chocolate."

She thought of Janie constantly. She wished Jane was with her right now, she would gladly buy her every treat she ever wanted.

8: Questions

Sam and Adam drove over to Trisha's apartment. They sat in the car for a long time, trying to see if anyone was watching them.

Adam entered the apartment building, sneaking a peek over his shoulder. Sam followed close behind. Adam knew Trisha would still be up waiting for him and that she would not be happy. He was sorry to disappoint her again. He was half scared that this time he had gone too far, and she was going to dump him and call the cops or, worse, call Thomas.

"Hey, baby, we need to talk," Adam said, aiming a kiss at the sleepy but angry-looking Trisha. She looked like she hadn't slept at all. Her red hair was in tangled curls from running her hands through it. Adam knew how much she played with her beautiful long curly hair when she was nervous. It was a lifelong habit. Trisha twirled her hair around her fingers all the time. Her hair was one of her best features.

"Where have you been all day and night? Why don't you answer your phone? I was so worried!" Trisha lowered her voice. "Word is Thomas is looking for you guys. Anyone who sees you is to call him right away. He is not happy." She looked scared. "I'll be in trouble if he finds out I talked to you and didn't call him."

"I'm sorry, Trish. I didn't want you or anyone else to get hurt," Adam said.

"How do you keep getting in so much trouble? You better clean up your act."

"I will, baby. This is the last fuck-up. If we can fix everything, I'm going straight after this. I'll go to rehab, a real one not the government-funded joke I tried the last time. NA, fuck, I'll even go to church if it will make you still love me. I will stop. I mean it this time."

"What did you do? Why is he after you? Why the hell didn't you stay away from Thomas? Let me guess, you needed the money for more drugs or to pay for the ones you already smoked. You know better, you asshole. You swore you would stop pulling this kind of shit."

"Sam and I were delivering a package for him. We had some time to kill before the drop, so we stopped for a drink. Figured we could be in and out of the club in a few minutes. We had a few drinks and lost track of time. You know how it goes. It slipped away."

"Do you mean last night? When we were partying like there was no tomorrow, you should have been working? For Thomas? I told you more than once not to get involved in Thomas' dirty little schemes." Trisha crushed out a cigarette and immediately lit another one. She puffed on it like she'd die if she stopped hauling.

"It's all my fault." Adam groaned. "If I would have stayed off the crack and booze, I wouldn't have gotten so fucked up and lost track of the bag. I was nervous, I had to do something for my nerves. I couldn't deal with the drop and that sad sack Sam."

"It's my fault, too. I smoked as much crack as you. I drank as much or more than you, too," Sam said from where he had perched on the counter. "What matters now is we find the drugs and get Jane back."

"Get Jane back?" Trisha sniffled and wiped away tears that were running down her cheek. "What do you mean?

Where is Jane?"

"Thomas or his goons took her. No reason for anyone else to have taken her. He wants his drugs back. If we don't find them, Jane is dead, and we will be too."

"How do you plan to find her or the drugs? What if they decide to come after me, too? Thomas knows I'm your girlfriend. He knows exactly where I live and work. How am I supposed to feel safe now? What am I going to do?"

"We were going to get you to ask around the club to see if anyone acting strange was around that night?"

"I don't know about that idea. It will make me more of a target. Thomas will know I talked to you. I can be discreet but some others at the club, not so much."

"You are right. Act like nothing is wrong. Don't tell him, or anyone else, you saw us today. Play dumb. Go to work as usual. Be a little down. Say it pisses you off that you haven't seen me for days, this is the last straw, and that you are gonna dump my junkie ass."

"Now that story sounds believable. It seems like something that could still happen." Trisha blew her nose into a tissue to try to hide a smile. "Wait, I have something for you."

She ran into the bedroom, he heard things being thrown around. Then she came out with something in a leather bag. "Here: take this. It was my Dad's. He was so proud of owning it. I was always afraid of it, so when he got forgetful I took it away and hid it so he wouldn't get hurt. You might need it."

Adam peered into the bag. A funky old handgun, like something from a cowboy movie, peered back at him. "Shit."

"Thomas and his people aren't playing, Adam."

He closed the bag carefully. "We will fix everything.

Don't worry. You will be fine and we are getting Jane back. Lynda, you go wait at the hotel."

His words sounded good, but they all knew the chances of all that happening were lower than dirt.

9: Scorned

Denise looked over her outfit for the night with a critical eye. She had to be fussy: her looks were how she made money.

This outfit was one of her favourites. Super-short black and silver latex dress, with lots of strategic holes to show off all her smooth curves. It fit like a second skin. Her shoes were super-tall spike heels. Her straight long brown hair had bright streaks of purple and blonde. Lots of black mascara covered her eyelashes. Smoky eye shadow, the right thing to bring out the evil sparkle in her brown eyes. Dark red lipstick and lots of glitter. Glitter everywhere.

They could call her a whore all they wanted, she didn't care. Glitter still made her feel like a princess. Everything came together to suit her to a T. Even after having a baby, she looked amazing.

She was ready to go to work. Her second set started just before midnight. The customers should be all li-quored up by then. Denise knew if she could get a couple of them in the VIP room she could make enough money to pay the rent. The landlady was ready to kick her and the baby out. She loved their place. If she had to live in this small town, that was the only place she wanted to stay.

Men branded women sluts and whores even when they didn't take their clothes off for money. A way to shame them into obedience. She started stripping because she figured she might as well have some money to go along with the name.

The first time she was called a whore she wasn't stripping, or dancing, or doing anything anyone else didn't do. She was walking down the street in broad daylight. Denise had been enjoying her day. Getting out of her tiny dorm room for a walk on the cobbled streets always lifted her spirits.

A black truck roared by. Some coward yelled "whore" out the window, from the safe darkness of black-tinted windows. He didn't even have the guts to show his face.

At first, she cried a bit. She thought about jumping off the bridge she had to cross to get back to her campus. There were rows and rows of train tracks under it, so if she timed it just right she could end it all pretty quick.

Then she decided to never let the judgment of others ever hurt her again. Denise took control. She moved here and started dancing and enjoying her body, not hiding it to please double-standard hypocritical prudes.

Denise checked to see if the old gym bag was still stuffed down in the bottom of the closet. Sitting under the huge pile of dirty clothes. Yup, it was still there. Good, she thought, and smiled a bitter smile. It looked like they had gotten away with it. She was sure Sam was somewhere squirming right now. Squirming and bleeding.

Denise didn't want to get Sam killed, but she wanted to make him hurt a lot. Wanted to crush him. Break him. Break his heart in little bitty pieces. Like he did when he left her and their son Michael. She had loved him so much, more than anything. There was no exact reason why, she just did. He didn't feel the same. He loved crack more.

He had the nerve to say she wasn't a good mother. That he wanted custody. Like she was gonna let that asshole and his new little bitch raise her son. He couldn't take care of the baby; he couldn't take care of himself. He was always looking for work, and when he found it wasn't long until he found a reason to quit or get fired. Same story every time. Someone there didn't like him and had it out for him, or the boss was a jerk. His back, neck or leg hurt, any one of a million excuses she was sick and tired of hearing. The truth was he couldn't hold a job because he partied too much, and he was lazy.

She kept working, Trisha helped her book time off, helped her find a place to go, and she went to rehab and cleaned up her act. It hadn't been easy.

Now her baby was what she lived her life for. Not crack. Not dancing. Not Sam. All she had needed was a little help to get on the right path, to find her strength. She was a good mother. Denise loved her son more than she ever loved Sam, more than she loved herself.

She wasn't sure exactly what to do with the stolen heroin. Just having it in the house made her nervous. It was like a ticking bomb, with a bunch of eights flashing on the timer. It could blow up in her face any second.

She knew what kind of person Thomas was. Not someone she wanted to be on the wrong side of. If she gave it back to him she would get nothing except lose her job and catch a beating for being a thief.

Maybe she could sell it to someone else and use the money to leave. Go far away from this dead-end place and people. Ugh. She hated them all. There was nothing to stay here for. No future. They needed a fresh new start where no one knew her as an ex crack user or former stripper. Sam would never be able to find her again or take Mikey away.

The heroin was her way out. If the choice was Micheal or Sam, there was no choice. She would always choose

Michael. Sam had made his choice the day he walked away from her.

10: Life's a dance

Trisha wondered where Adam was right now. She was worried about him. He and Sam were in big trouble. They had to lay low until they could fix their problems with Thomas. She liked Jane and hoped she was all right.

It had been a pretty quiet night so far at the club. Usually, the place got more exciting after midnight. A pair of dancers were finishing their set. As the tall redhead and leggy blonde left the stage, she realized she hadn't seen Denise arrive. It was almost time for her to go on. Trisha wasn't surprised that Denise wasn't here yet. She was always late. One of those people who was always in such a hurry that they never arrived anywhere on time. Always running around stressing herself out.

Thomas was watching her from the office doorway. He filled the door frame pretty much completely. He never came in this early. Trisha smiled and waved at him. She had known Thomas for years. Even on a good day, he never smiled. Unless he got to show off his muscles; that usually made him smile. He was good to have around the club. Just looking at him made most people settle down. Thomas was a good manager, kept the place running. He didn't own the place, but she knew he wanted to.

Thomas barely nodded at her. His eyes drifted back to the stage as strains of "You Better Run" by Motorhead poured out of the speakers.

Denise flowed out onto the stage with her long shimmering hair swirling all around her. She was good at her job. Really good. There was a reason she was a dancer. She was made for it. Denise always drew a nice crowd. She danced like fire on the stage, and everyone in the place wanted to get burned. You didn't have to be a man either; women loved watching her dance too. She was perfect.

She was looking better than ever since she had cleaned up her act. When she had found out she was pregnant, she had gotten off crack and took care of herself and of her baby. She was going to school, too. She was a nice girl. She had made some bad decisions in her life, but who hadn't? She learned from her mistakes and tried to do better. It's all anyone could do.

Some of the girls were extra-talented and pretty hot acts. A mix of acrobat skills and fire. It got the crowd going. Sex mixed with fire couldn't get any hotter. The nights they were on, all the girls made extra cash, all the guys too. Bouncers, bartenders and dancers. Everyone got what they wanted. They only had the special shows a few times a year. It was good to make them wait, and wait and want. They would get bored and broke if they could see a show like that every night.

Thomas didn't usually pay much attention to the girls. She wondered if Tom was lonely or horny tonight. Who knew? He wasn't the sort to confide his deepest desires to her. Trisha was too worried about Adam to think about it too much. She hoped the boys would all play nice and work their shit out.

Maybe Thomas and Denise would hook up. A good piece of tail might do them both some good. She must have been working here too long, for her mind to go to the bedroom as a solution. She had learned young that people had sex, that was just what they did. Even when they shouldn't, they sought each other out. This was the kind of dark place they found each other.

A young woman in a short navy blue dress, smiling and waving at her, interrupted Trisha's train of thought. "Excuse me. Hi, hellooo, anybody home? Can a girl get some beer and drinks?"

"Sorry, I was off in my own little world. Sure, coming right up. Keith's draft or bottle?"

"Bottles, and two doubles of Crown Royal too, please. Not very busy yet, guess we picked the right time to stop by. The gang won't have to compete for the dancers' attention."

There was just one table occupied by more than one person, two guys and another pretty girl. The rest of the patrons were loners drinking beer and watching the stage. These guys must be big spenders, Trisha thought. They already had two dancers at their table. "Easy to get the dancers' attention, just wave some money at them, they will flock to your table."

"That sounds like a plan for a good night."

"Enjoy your drinks and the ladies."

"We will."

Trisha wished the night would end so she could talk to Adam. She missed him.

11: Heating up

The phone behind the bar rang again. It had been ringing half the night. No one paid any attention. You could barely even hear it over the music, maybe between songs, but you could see a little light flash when it rang.

Denise was dancing her second set of the night. She was killing it, as usual. The crowd was pretty lively for a weeknight. They were cheering, whistling, and laughing, and everyone seemed to be having a great time.

The phone rang, and rang again. Trish looked at the bartender, Alice, who was elbow deep in loud drunks. She wasn't going to be able to answer the phone, even if she wanted to. Alice was running both bars and doing a good job of it by the look of her overflowing tip jar. If she dropped her guard even for a second, though, she would get groped for sure. Then someone's fingers were going to get smashed. It had happened before. None of the ladies who worked at Pleasures took any shit, from each other or from the customers.

Trish squeezed past Max, the other bartender. By the time she reached the phone it had stopped ringing again. She slammed the receiver back down. She should have known.

Ring, ring it started again almost immediately. For Christ's sake, who was calling here and hanging up? Some passed off wife or girlfriend? It wouldn't be the first time.

She grabbed the phone again. "What?" she yelled into the receiver.

All she could hear was a baby crying. "Hello, is anybody there? Who's calling? I don't have time to fuck around. Hello?!"

"Hi, I'm calling for Denise," a timid female voice said. There was so much noise in the bar Trish almost didn't hear her, but she could hear the baby crying.

Denise was spinning on the pole, a little too busy to come to the phone. Though if Denise wanted to talk on the phone while she danced, there were probably people here who would love to pay to watch her do it. People would pay to watch her do a lot of things.

"Denise is busy right now, honey. Can she call you back? Do you want to leave a message?"

"It's Amie, I'm taking care of Michael. I think he has a fever, he won't stop crying. Denise said the baby Motrin was in the diaper bag, but I can't find it."

"Okay, hon, I'll see what I can do. Don't worry. I'll get Denise to call you back in a few minutes."

Trisha hung up the phone, a little upset. That kid needed something to break the fever. Poor Amie, she was barely twelve. She shouldn't be taking care of a sick baby. Denise was usually better than this, but everybody forgot things sometimes, especially when babies cried. Trisha just hoped this wasn't a sign that Denise had started to slip into crack again.

Denise was just walking off the stage. Trisha caught up with her in the dressing room. "Hey, Den, Amie called about Mikey. She can't find the Motrin."

"Oh, fuck! I thought I put it in his bag in case they needed it. Fuck! I'm so stupid!" Denise buried her head in her hands.

"Do you have some at home? I can probably sneak

away for a few minutes easier than you can."

"Thank you, Trisha, thank you from Mikey!" Denise gave her a sweaty, glitter-covered hug. "That would be so great, are you sure you don't mind?"

"Not a problem."

"The crowd is pretty excited tonight, must be a full moon or something. I'm making great tips. We could really use the money."

She closed her eyes for a second, visualizing. "I'm sure there is a brand-new bottle of Motrin in the spare diaper bag in the bathroom. I'll give you the keys if you want to run over and get it."

Denise said, "Okay, I'll go grab it and drop it off for you. I'll have a peek at Michael. Where are Amie and Mikey staying?"

Denise was putting on an outfit for her next dance, a dress that was mostly black fringe that moved when she did. She was good at choosing clothes to suit her best features. "They are at my sister Carla's place, over on the New Road. Do you know where she lives?"

"Oh yes, I've been there before. It's a short trip, won't take me long at all. You won't even miss me."

Denise hugged her again. "Thank you, Trish, you really are a lifesaver. I'll call Amie and let her know you are coming. Give Mikey a hug and a kiss for me and tell him Mama will be home soon to cuddle with her baby boy."

"I will." Trisha said.

"They are playing my song." Denise said with a grin as she ran for the stage.

Trisha grabbed her keys and went to take care of someone else's mess. If it didn't involve a kid, she would have said no, but Mikey was so sweet. She also wanted to have a quick look around the apartment and make sure Denise was staying off crack. She loved her kid but being a single mom stripper wasn't easy, and there was temptation all around. High stress, it was a job some girls need help to do. Some turned to booze, some turned to drugs, and some loved every bit of it.

If Denise needed a little extra support, Trisha would do her best to help. She couldn't make people stop taking drugs. If they wanted to get high, they would find a way. Her own uncle would huff gas or glue if he couldn't get alcohol, acid or at least some weed. Denise wouldn't be the first girl she helped to point in the right direction. Some didn't take the help she offered, and that was fine, but she didn't refuse anyone who was trying.

She hadn't heard from Adam all night, but this trip would distract her for a little while. A 20-minute drive one way. She cranked the radio and sang along with the hair metal songs she had always loved.

Trisha pulled into the driveway of the duplex where Denise and Mikey lived. The other half of the house looked empty. It was a nice place in a good neighbourhood. It seemed like Denise really had turned her life around when she left Sam. Trisha hoped appearances matched reality.

She used the key Denise gave her to unlock the front door. Everything looked great, clean and neat, with lots of food in the fridge. Den was a great housekeeper, cleaning was always the last thing on Trisha's to-do list.

She continued through the house toward the bathroom. She dug in the closet to find the diaper bag. Opened the bag to see if there was any Motrin in it and fished out a bottle that looked like medicine. It said "gripe water". Nope, not it. She was glad to put it back, she hated the black licorice smell.

Trisha found a second small bottle. Her eyesight wasn't that great, especially without her glasses, but she saw an "M". Yes! This had to be the stuff.

She went to shove it back into the diaper bag and bring the whole thing to Amie, but the bottle slipped out of her fingers and fell down to the bottom of the closet, in among some dirty towels.

Shit! All she needed was to dig through a stripper's dirty laundry. Fuck it, it was for baby Mikey.

Trisha got down on her knees and started to dig around. This was taking forever. She had thought she'd be done and back behind the bar already, enjoying herself even more than she was now by wiping up spilled beer and glitter. At least they couldn't smoke in the bar anymore, that was one less thing to clean up.

She was gonna have to take everything out to find the bottle. She pulled a couple big clumps of old towels and baby clothes out and threw them on the bathroom floor. The last pile seemed to be stuck, so she pulled harder.

A funky sports bag tumbled out with the damp towels and something heavy hit the ceramic tiles. She found the little bottle of baby medicine in the back corner of the closet and then went to see what she had knocked on the floor. She hoped there was nothing breakable.

The zipper wasn't closed all the way, and she could see what was in the bag. She could not believe her eyes. Bricks of something, probably coke or heroin. THE fucking heroin. Why did Denise have it? What the fuck was going on?

She quickly stuffed the baby's medicine in her purse, then went to the kitchen to find a garbage bag. She found one under the kitchen sink. It didn't take long to transfer the heroin to the plastic bag. She stuck a few dirty towels in the sports bag, zipped it up and shoved it into the bottom of the closet, then covered it with the rest of the laundry.

Now to drop off the baby's medicine, then go find Denise and kick her ass.

She tried to call Adam, but his phone was off. The battery on his crappy ancient iPhone had probably died. Trisha texted Sam, too, but got no reply. She needed to find them, and hoped it wasn't too late.

No choice but to hide the heroin until she knew Jane and the guys were safe. She wished she knew where they were.

This was Thomas' bag, but she couldn't give it up too soon or things wouldn't end well for Adam. Fucking heroin, fucking Thomas.

What the fuck was Denise doing with the bag? Trisha knew Denise's relationship with Mikey's Dad wasn't great, but shit like this would get someone killed.

12: Darkness

Jane opened her eyes and blinked. She couldn't see anything at all—her eyes were covered. Everything was black
as the inside of a stovepipe. Great.

What was in her mouth, a gag? She tried to spit it out,
but no luck. She wished she could have a drink. Anything
to change the awful taste in her mouth. She felt so tired,
why did she feel so bad? She had a splitting headache.
Where was she?

She tried to scream, but a muffled "mmmmfff" squeak
is all that came out.

She succeeded in making herself feel more lightheaded
and a lot like throwing up. It was a feeling she seemed to
have a lot lately. Staying calm was not easy. Her mind was
screaming, and spinning, even if she wasn't making any
noise at all.

Besides the blindfold and gag, strong ropes kept her in
the hard chair she was sitting in.

She tried to fight the groggy feeling, still feeling like
she might be sick. That wouldn't be good with a gag in
her mouth. She tried to focus her mind and slowed her
breathing down; it helped a bit. A few more slow breaths
as deep as possible through her nose made her head feel
a little better.

The last thing she could remember was answering a
knock at the door at her friend Tara's apartment. She had
been staying there for the last little while while Tara was

gone home to visit her parents for a couple of weeks. Perfect timing, or, so she had thought at the time. She had wanted some time to herself to think about the future.

Now she found herself a prisoner in total darkness. What was going on? She tried to loosen the ropes: no dice. The ropes almost seemed to get tighter the more she squirmed. Whoever had tied the knots knew what they were doing. A real boy scout.

Jane listened, it was quiet. No traffic, no dogs barking or kids playing. All she could hear was her own frantic heartbeat. She wished she had someone to talk to, with this gag in she couldn't even talk to herself.

She passed out again wondering what in the world was going on and how she was going to get out of here.

Jane awoke, less groggy than before but still confined to the hard chair in the dark, to the sound of tires crunching on gravel. She had no idea how long she had been there. It had been quite a while, judging by how badly she had to pee. She hoped someone would come soon. If not, things would get messy, fast.

She heard a key in the lock. There were two voices outside the door. They didn't talk much, and the sound was muffled, but she thought the voices belonged to two men. She would know soon. She had wanted someone to talk to, looked like it was time to get her wish.

Jane put her head down and pretended she was still asleep.

13: The job

It was peaceful outside the cabin by the river. It wasn't really a cabin; the boss called it 'the cabin', but it was more like a house. A big house. It had lots of bedrooms, two bathrooms, a hot tub, a sauna, a fireplace. The works. From the outside, it looked like a nice family getaway. Complete with flower beds, monstrous lilac bushes, and a tire swing hanging from an old oak tree. The little covered porch and neat yard looked friendly and inviting. The paint was a little faded but could last another year or two before being painted. It wasn't the kind of place you would expect to find a hostage or drug dealers.

"Don't you know how to use a key, Bobby?" Jim said.

"Just gimme a minute. Keep it down, will ya?"

"If you would hurry up and open the damn door I wouldn't have to keep it down."

"It's not like there's anyone else out here anyway. I'll get it."

"Come on, give me the key." Jim snatched the key and jammed it in the lock. He tried to turn it: nothing. It was jammed.

"See?" Bob said. "Guess you aren't the locksmith you think you are." He reached out and tried to snatch the key back out of the lock.

"Watch it there, greenhorn. Didn't your Mama teach you any manners?" Jim said, slapping Bobby's hand away like an annoying mosquito. "I still have a few tricks up my sleeve."

He pulled the doorknob towards the frame, kicked the bottom corner and tried the key again. There was a little click.

"Bingo!" he smiled his ugly little smile. God, how Bobby hated that smile. "Old places like this move around when the ground freezes and thaws every year. Sometimes the doors jam; so you gotta put a little more work into it."

Still grinning, Jim stepped back and held the door open. "After you, rookie."

"Thanks, old man," Bob said, wearing an almost ugly grin to match Jim's. He knew it wasn't a friendly one, either. Kinda like a smiley Bob mask. He was never that good at hiding his emotions. His face always wanted to give him away. If he could have seen himself, he might have been a little frightened. He reminded himself to do his job better, to show the boss what he could do. Or he would forever be doing shit jobs with jerks like Jim. Or even worse, more jobs with Jim. Now that would be hell. One more job with Jim telling him what to do every five seconds would make him blow his own brains out.

Bob was young, but he wasn't a rookie. He had been down more than a few dirt roads. Jim didn't know the shit he'd been party to, didn't mean he was any less of a bad-ass. Jim was in the dark about who was smarter and tougher than who in this delightful duo. Bob was ready to climb the ladder. Jim would always be on the bottom rung. Someone you step over.

Bob had to prove to everyone that he wasn't a nice guy. In this line of business you didn't get to the top by being a nice guy. You had to be ruthless and willing to do what others aren't willing to. Going to longer lengths to get what you wanted, and being able to keep it, was proof that you deserved it. When he got what he wanted, he held on tight with both hands. He would be the one who got respect. No more being a lackey for anyone.

14: Worth a thousand words

The door opened and closed with a soft click. She heard two sets of heavy footsteps cross the room. Her vision lit up like fireworks when someone slapped her hard and said, "Wake up, honey, it's time to have a little talk."

She made a weak sound. It kind of sounded like a cross between "why" and a moan.

"What? What was that darlin'?" A man's voice said. He sounded like he was smiling. She was glad she couldn't see his face.

Several more quick slaps. Her head spun. If she wouldn't have been tied to the chair, she would have fallen off of it.

"I can't hear you. Speak clearer, bitch," the same mean voice laughed. Almost giggled. The gleeful malice in his voice shocked her even more than the slaps. What did she ever do to him? He was having a great time, like he got his happy hands on a shiny new toy.

"Take out the fuckin' gag first, why don't ya, Jim?" a different voice said. "Come on, ya yahoo, think about it. Maybe she will be a little more cooperative, you might get a few words out of her." He didn't sound like he was enjoying things as much as the first thug.

"Fuck you, Bobby! Don't try to tell me how to do my job, kid. I've been in the game since you were in shitty diapers."

Jim turned his attention back to Jane, like a dog gnawing on a bone. "I always had a weakness for blondes, especially with such long hair." He brushed a few strands of her honey-blonde hair away from her face. If you ignored the ropes and blindfold, it was sweet.

Jane cringed and pulled away from his touch. That wasn't so sweet. The touch was soft, but to see how fast she pulled away, his fingers might as well have been hot metal.

"I could have a lot of fun with her. A lot of fun." He pulled the rag out of her mouth and slapped Jane again. This time he split her lip open, and she screamed. The sharp sound cut through the quiet room like a knife. Blood ran down her chin. Her mouth filled with the hot coppery taste of her own blood.

Jim laughed again. You could hear the joy in it. Good thing someone was having fun around here. Jane wondered again what was going on, why she was here, and if she would ever leave this place.

They hit her again. Then the one called Bobby said, "That's enough for now. The boss said to call this number, rough her up a bit and text a photo to those idiots. This should clear things up for them. Once the boss gets what he wants from them, you'll be able to get what you want from her. You can tie up the loose ends any way you want, when the boss says so."

She tried not to react to their words. She could tell they were trying to get a rise out of her. It almost worked. She was terrified but held her tongue.

Bobby's voice came closer to her for the first time. His dry lips were touching her ear. Jane tried to move away from his hot breath. She couldn't get away. The ropes held her immobile. She wanted to vomit.

"Smile for the birdie." Jane heard a little click beep of a cell phone camera. "This should get an answer out of those two little pricks. You'd better hope they surface soon, honey, or Jim here might get to indulge in his fondness for blondes."

This time both men laughed.

Jane thought it was her perspective, but she didn't think anything about this situation was funny. She didn't feel like laughing as she ran her tongue over the busted skin on the inside of her swollen lips. She tried to spit out the blood, but even that hurt.

What had she ever done to anyone to deserve this? They never even asked her any questions. Not even one. If they had, she might have some idea of what the hell was going on. She tried not to panic. They were looking for two idiots. That sounded a lot like her ex, Sam, and the ever-fucking-present Adam. What had those two morons gotten her into? If she ever got out of here, she was going to kill them herself. This shit was exactly why she had left Sam.

Sam would never change, no matter what he told her. He said the words she wanted to hear, over and over, but they had no meaning. He would lie to her to get what he wanted. Beautiful, heartbreaking lies. All the "I'm sorry's" that were just words he said, that he didn't even hear himself.

The bad times were quickly outweighing the good ones. It was getting harder to remember the good. Jane wished, not for the first time, that she had never met Sam.

15: Leave a message

"You got the number ready?" Jim said.

"Yeah, I have it."

"Call it. No sense wasting any more time. I wanna get to bed before dawn."

Bob touched in the numbers and pressed *send*. It rang quite a few times. No answer. He hung up when it went over to the message machine.

He watched Jim hit Jane a few more times. Seemed to be enjoying himself; her, not so much. It didn't faze Bob, it was like watching a movie on TV. He'd seen worse things happen. He'd done worse. Bob wasn't into slapping women around. He would do what the boss told him to, although he was glad to be the one holding the phone, not the one doing the beating. No fun in beating up someone who couldn't fight back. A little slap and tickle in the bedroom with willing participants was fun. A good fistfight, now that was something Bob liked. When Thomas said jump, Bob said "How high?" He wanted to move up in the business. He had to prove he could get the job done.

"No answer. Those pussies are too scared to answer their fucking phone. What should we do Jimmy, leave the deadbeats a little message?"Jim smiled one of his evil smiles. "Call them again. If they don't answer this time, the lovely Miss Jane here will leave a nice, short message for us."

Bobby pressed *send* again. Still no answer. No surprise.

"All right blondie, you know how it works, leave a message after the beep."

He held the phone up to her mouth as the beep came through. In a cracked, shaky dry voice Jane spoke "Please someone, help m—"

Jim cut her off with a couple hard smacks, then more, and even a few more. She screamed more wordless screams, then hung her head and sobbed.

He didn't even raise his voice when he spoke. He didn't have to. "You know what we want. Meet us with our package or soon she won't be making any more noise. I'll be calling again. You'd better answer when I do, or else." Jim slapped Jane, like an exclamation mark that echoed in the room and Bob hung up.

Bob shoved the gag back in Jane's mouth. He bent down and buried his entire face in her hair, pushing his lips right up against her ear. She could feel his hot breath on her skin as he whispered, "Good job, sweetie. We gotta go look for your loser boyfriend. We won't be gone for long, so don't try nothing funny, there is no one around here for forty miles. You needn't bother wasting your time screaming or trying to hitch a ride. No one ever comes back here. This is the big woods. You leave this house and all you'll find outside are hungry wild animals. They'll eat you up even faster than ol' Jimmy here."

He followed the other man out the door, both of them still laughing.

16: The right thing

Captain MacDonald was so mad his face was way past red, it was a very dark shade of purple. He hadn't taken a breath in so long John was starting to worry he was going to pass out or have a heart attack.

"Look, Detective, you'll do as I say, or you will lose what little job you have left. You might think you are some big shot coming down here from the city, going to show us how to do our jobs. Try to make us look like a bunch of stupid hicks. We know your kind around here. Do the job I tell you to do or find the door."

"I am trying to do my job, sir."

"No. You are trying to do what you want. You don't run this place. I do. I choose who gets what case. Do you know how much money we wasted setting up that bust that never happened? How many man-hours I can't get back? That was your bright idea. It better be your last."

"Okay, okay. I hear you. You're the boss," John said.

"No piece of shit drunk driver is going to tell me how to run my detachment. You don't have the best reputation for making good decisions. I am the one who makes *all* the decisions around here. I told you to solve some of the break-ins and car thefts, and the multiple open cases of arson. I don't want to see you in my office again until you solve a case! Now get out!"

John got up and left without another word. He hated being here as much as they hated having him here.

He went back to his office and sat down. He rubbed his burning, tired eyes. He had been staring at the case files all night. Like he always did. Well, one case file in particular. He took a swallow of coffee that had been made ages ago and winced at the foul, bitter taste. He hated cold coffee, time for a refill.

Before he could get up and head to the probably empty coffee maker, his desk phone buzzed. "Hey John, we got a worried lady here who says her little sister is missing," Tina said. The only friendly face in the whole detachment. She was still young; it would take a few years on the job to make her cynical and jaded as the rest of them.

Great, just what he needed. A dead-end missing persons case, like he didn't have enough cases on his plate that were going nowhere.

"Can't someone else take it? Where the hell is the rookie?"

"We're short-handed because of the long weekend. Everyone here is already busy or at home sleeping." He could hear her smile "Looks like you are all we got left. Besides, the Captain said to give it to you. Sorry Johnny, I'm just doing what I'm told."

Of course the Captain did. Ol' Johnny Boy was on the shit list, with no way to ever get off it. Like he wasn't busy, too, and already way past overtime.

Ah well, he hoped the missing person was sleeping off a drunk somewhere. With any luck, they would turn up in a few hours missing a shoe, broke, with a bad hangover. He might as well start the paperwork. There was always more paperwork to do, no matter what case he worked on. He did more paperwork than actual police work, maybe that's how the bad guys kept one step ahead, they didn't fuck around with paperwork. "Alright, gimme two minutes and show her in. I'll do what I can."

He was a good cop. He just fell asleep. He had been working undercover, living a double life. He took a few uppers now and then to help stay up, booze to come down. On the way home one night he fell asleep at the wheel, crashed into a young family on their way home from a night at the movies. A child died at the scene. He hadn't been out drinking and partying; he had one beer with his supper that night. It didn't matter. He was supposed to protect people, not kill them.

The rest of the precinct shunned him, they gossiped and talked, and what they didn't know they made up. To them he was a cop who couldn't handle the job. Stories that he enjoyed his undercover work more than his real life. That he was going though a divorce and coping by hitting the bottle. There was even talk of a nervous breakdown. Some of it was true, and some wasn't. Like all situations, there was a lot of grey. In the end, the divorced part was true.

They didn't fire him, he had too many years on the job and too many friends in high places. Cops never got fired for fucking up. Kinda like priests, they get sent to a new place far away. They sent him here, the other end of the country to middle-of-nowhere Nova Scotia to finish out his years behind a desk until his pension kicked in. Maybe then he could go live on a beach down south. No one would know him there. It couldn't happen soon enough. He kept hoping for a good case to come across his desk so he could retire on a good note. So far, nothing.

He took a quick last glance at the photos spread out across his desk. Lots of low-level dealers, but the boss was still hiding. He had to stop these guys. They were the ones flooding the province with heroin. He would have bet money that they'd have gotten something out of the drop the other night. But they didn't show. Couldn't bust half a drug deal. Somehow they must have gotten tipped off it was a setup. Had they spotted a tail? Did someone warn them off? He wished he knew who or what had clued them in, so he could make sure it didn't happen again.

The Captain had been so pissed, he pulled all the guys off the case. He told John to leave it alone. Fuck the Captain. He would keep watching the scum on his own time and try to get the next shipment. There was always another parcel, package or shipment. It never ended. Even when he caught these guys, he knew there would be someone waiting to make up the slack and fill the void. There would be a lineup of faceless someones waiting and willing to take the job.

Some days he thought he was fighting a losing battle. Most days, as of late. It never ended. No wonder cops burnt out. Never-ending criminals.

But he couldn't give up. The job was his whole life, he had to keep this shit off the streets. After all he had kids to think about, even if they never thought about him.

He would get these scumbags and put them away. He wanted the boss, the one at the top, the one who profited most from the misery of the users. The delivery boys had no pull or say in anything. He'd sweep them up too, if he could, but the bosses, the guys at the top, were the ones John wanted. They were vultures, or worse, like a pack of rats picking away at cripples who can't protect themselves. Stealing a tiny piece at a time until there was nothing recognizable left.

Instead of getting help, most users ended up in jail or homeless. Help was hard to get. So much fear of addiction and mental illness existed, it was hard to get others to see the truth, that the users were the real victims. All he could do as a cop was try to stop the people who were providing the heroin, crack, coke, meth and all the rest.

All the rest...more new addictive drugs hit the streets every day. It was hard to keep up with the names, let alone stop the flow. Plenty of them were prescription drugs doctors handed out like candy, too. Pills made the world go round. It was up to the government to fix the system. The system that has pretty much always been broken. He couldn't really fight it. He was a little wheel, after all.

A knock on the door cut his train of thought short. He called, "Just a second," swept the photos into the folder marked "Heroin" and put it in his top drawer. He locked the drawer and dropped the key back into his pocket. He kept the file close even though he didn't need to look at it; he had memorized every bit of info in it. He knew every word, every line, by heart. John had to have missed something. He still didn't know who the top dog was.

"All right," he said to the door. It opened and in walked a short, pretty, but tired-looking brunette who looked like she had seen far better days.

17: Reaching out

John stood and stuck out his hand over the piles of files, folders, and crumpled papers on his desk. "Hello Ma'am, how can I help you? My name is Detective John Tower. Please have a seat, Mrs...?"

"Lynda Roberts. Please, call me Lynda." She shook his hand.

"Okay, Lynda it is. Whatever makes you feel more comfortable. Go ahead, tell me your story." He couldn't help thinking her hands were so soft.

"Detective, I need your help. Well, not me, it's my sister, Jane. She needs your help. She's missing."

"If I'm going to call you Lynda, you might as well call me John." He smiled "You can call me anything you want, just don't call me late for supper."

"Sure, then John it is. Thanks, Can you help me find my sister?"

"We will do everything we can to help you. Are you sure Jane is not out with a friend or took a weekend shopping trip on the spur of the moment?"

"She wouldn't take off without telling me. She always answers my texts and messages. Always. We talk or text pretty much every day. She's not a big shopper. We don't have any other family, it's just us, and we are very close. "

"Did you and your sister have a fight?

"No. Never."

"Are you sure? Does she have a boyfriend?"

"Yes."

"Did they have a fight?"

"No—yes. All that doesn't matter. You aren't listening to me. My sister needs your help. I hope we can find her in time."

"I am not trying to be difficult, Lynda, I am trying to understand why you think she is missing. What if she doesn't want anyone to find her? She is a grown woman. There are some things you aren't telling me. I can only help you if you tell me everything you know about the situation. Why do you think Jane is in danger?"

"If I tell you everything I can, will you help my sister?" She grabbed his big hand with her small shaking one.

"I'll do my best to help you. That's what I do. Help people. Let's sit and see what we can figure out. Would you like some coffee? I can't promise you it will be good, but it will be strong and hot."

"Thank you, coffee and a talk sounds great."

18: Lady Luck

John couldn't believe his luck. There was no way to explain it other than pure luck. He didn't believe in destiny. He was sure this missing person case was the key to cracking the drug ring he had been investigating for months. All the extra unpaid hours he put in this case, with no results, and out of the blue the answer falls right into his lap. At first, he had thought this case would be a waste of his time. Boy, was he wrong.

It wasn't a missing person case at all. It was a kidnapping of a drug dealer's girlfriend case. He bet if he could find this girl, he would find the kingpin behind everything. Orders for something big had to come from the top.

John asked questions, listened, made notes. He nodded at all the right places as Lynda spoke about her little sister. While she spoke, his mind raced, trying to figure how to use the situation to his and the Department's advantage. It could help the whole community. There were dirty needles all over the place: in parks, by the community mailboxes, just lying on the side of the road.

John said, "The first thing we have to do is talk to your sister's boyfriend." He checked his notes. "If Sam co-operates with my investigation, we should be able to find your sister."

"What do you mean 'co-operate'?" Lynda said. "What does Sam have to say and do? I'm sure he loves my sister, but he is such a fuck-up. In the short time I've known Sam I've learned the less you expect of him, the better."

"This is serious business. He will have to tell us everything. Who he was working for, who was he selling the drugs to. Anyone he talked to or saw or at the meetings. We have to find him now. These things usually escalate fast. Do you know where he is? Can you have him meet us somewhere?"

"I'll try his cell." She dug her phone out of her bag and dialed Sam's number. No answer. She hung up. "I'll try again in a few minutes." She threw the phone back into her purse.

The detective wondered how much Sam knew and if he could get him to spill everything about the operation. Even if he was low on the ladder he could lead them to someone bigger. Sam was going to have to stick his neck out. He would have to wear a wire and testify.

John hoped they would be able to find the girl, but his focus was stopping the flow of hard drugs. If a junkie like Sam got hurt along the way, John wouldn't feel too bad. Sam had made his own bed, so he'd have to live with it.

The way Lynda told the story, Jane didn't do drugs at all. Not even pot. She didn't smoke crack with Sam and his friends. Didn't even smoke cigarettes. John doubted that. He bet she was as bad as Sam and the rest of them. Just because big sister didn't know, didn't mean it wasn't true.

Maybe he was being too cynical. After everything he'd seen in his years on and off the force, he knew the truth usually wasn't pretty. It was almost always ugly, like an old witch hovering over a boiling cauldron.

Good thing his wife was an ex. He didn't have to call her to explain why he wouldn't be coming home for dinner again tonight.

19: Weight room

The phone rang. Thomas took his time to put down the barbell he was lifting, stretched his arms and back, then picked up the cell. It was tiny in his huge hands. It almost looked like a toy. He hated it when a good workout was interrupted. Fuck! He would almost have to start all over again. Just when he was getting into it, too.

Screwing with his sets always put him in a bad mood. Every time he went he swore he would not bring the phone into the gym with him, but he always did. He told himself he'd turn it off when he got inside, but he never did. He was afraid to miss something important. If Lewis needed him and he didn't answer, he would never hear the end of it. Either way, he was on the losing end. It was wearing on him. Lewis was getting more and more dependent on him lately, and Tom didn't want to babysit an old man.

"Yeah?" He growled into the phone.

"Have you solved the problem?" a calm but hard voice asked.

Great, it was Lewis. Again. He should have expected the call. Even though he already talked to him half a dozen times this morning. He eased the bass rumble in his voice a bit. He couldn't change it much and answered Lewis in a calm, polite tone. "Working on it, boss. It's in the works. Everything will be fine."

"People are waiting, and they don't enjoy waiting. It costs me money, it costs you money. Waiting costs everyone money."

"I know and things are finally moving along. I've got a plan. It's in motion already. This situation is not as bad as it seems, it's a little hiccup."

"You'd better get things under control. This 'little hiccup' is fucking with my bottom line. Worse than that, it is fucking with my credibility in the business. If I got no credibility, I got no respect, then me or some of my guys end up dead in a field somewhere. Fix this now."

"You gotta take it easy, boss. Just relax. We will have what we want very soon."

He stopped speaking. He was talking to dead air.

Thomas hated being dismissed like a servant. Lewis was always in a hurry when money was involved, and with Lewis, money was always involved.

He put down the phone and started lifting the weights again, then he stopped, grabbed the phone and turned it off. He needed time to think. If the boss kept nagging him he'd never get this figured out.

Thomas resumed his workout, letting the effort fuel his thinking. He had to make some calls and see if everything was going according to plan. It better be: they didn't want him to get mad. People got hurt when he got mad. If those two idiots fucked this situation up any worse, they would have to answer to Lewis for it, and so would he.

As much as he wanted the old man's job, he was happy with running things from the back seat for now. Thomas had to bide his time. The opportunity to take over the business would arise. When it did he would be ready.

Thomas almost went into a trance, he was concentrating so hard on using his muscles and counting the reps. It was like meditation. He felt like things would settle down. The boys could handle it from here.

After he finished his workout, he would check on things with Jim and Bob. He could tweak the plan a little according to what was taking place.

20: Lewis

Lewis hung up while Thomas was still talking. He never said bye. Hello wasn't a word he used much either. Waste of time. Words he liked to say most often were more like "my fucking money" and "now".

It's hard to find good fucking help. He supposed he should give Thomas a little slack. He didn't lose the package, but he hired the two morons who did. He hoped Thomas could fix this mess. Someone had to pay for this. No one messed with Lewis. He had a reputation to uphold.

At his age, he tried harder to stay under the radar. He had learned it was best to hide back in the shadows. He kept his head down, usually between a pair of beautiful, perky breasts. Thomas was the visible one who took care of the day to day. Thomas kept to himself, too. It was easier that way.

They had to get a handle on this situation. A mess like this could send the message that Lewis was weak. That he was getting old. If things appeared to be out of control in the community, it didn't look good for business. The last thing he needed was the competition or the cops crawling around his place.

He'd been spending more time at the doctor's office over the last year. Tests and more tests; he must have taken every test known to mankind. They could have even slipped a pregnancy test in there, and he wouldn't have known the difference. Some doctors were so dumb they'd have to run a test to figure out why he had a negative result on a pregnancy test. It always baffled him how such well-educated people could be so stupid most of the time.

Nurses were a whole different story. They were smarter and knew how to treat people. The doctors got a big paycheque and all the glory. And they said drug dealers were crooked.

One more round of tests and they'd know. It was the same old story. He didn't need the tests, he already knew it was lung cancer. He'd been coughing up blood for a while.

He'd done a good job of keeping it to himself. Lewis had a great poker face but knew his time was running out. That was why this Adam/Sam situation was so frustrating. He was trying to keep things in order and go out on top. He didn't have kids to leave this business to, but was the crew he had good enough to carry on without his guidance?

Lewis was planning a little vacation to sunny, green Costa Rica. Once this was all settled he was going away, for good. He didn't want to worry about this shit when he left. Once he headed off into the sunset, all the problems would belong to someone else. He would drink rum on a beach and roast in the sun until his last breath.

Thomas had to prove his intelligence, determination, and grit to make this right. Being the big dog in the yard was something you had to prove over and over. There was always some new hotshot trying to to take over and do whatever they want and not follow the rules. Show them the error of their ways fast, and be ready for the next sneak attack from the shadows.

He had expected Thomas to take things over for him in

time, but now he wasn't so sure. This had been a simple assignment. One that Thomas did a few times a month. For the last decade, it had all been running smooth as silk. If Thomas couldn't handle this little hiccup, then he definitely couldn't handle it all.

Maybe it was time for Lew to clean house and start up a fresh crew before the Costa Rica trip, so he could leave a good legacy. Or at least the illusion of one. Once he was dead, he wouldn't care one way or the other, but for now he still did.

21: Circles

Sam and Adam left Trisha's place and figured they had better crash for a while. They had been up for at least two days already. Trisha would text them as soon as she heard anything. They hadn't slept and had a long night ahead of them.

Sam wished he had a hit. *Fuck, fuck, why did I ever start?* The want, the need, gnawed at his brain. He wanted to crawl right out of his skin. When you smoked crack, everything was great. When you ran out, that was a different story.

He still remembered the very first time. It wasn't very long ago, a couple of months. With Adam and Trisha; Jane had been there too. It was the best. It felt so damn good. He had tried every other drug (except needle drugs, he had to draw the line somewhere). Cigarettes, booze, grass, mushrooms, hash, acid, speed, coke, powders, potions, and prescription pills, too. But this, this was the one thing that made him feel the best. Nothing else in the world made him feel so good. When he had it.

He glanced over at Adam all twitchy and restless in the passenger seat, picking at a rip in his dirty jeans. Sam wondered if they could score a hit somewhere, a tiny rock would make them both feel good. Sam knew better, but he couldn't stop himself.

"Hey, Adam, you got any friends who could front us a rock or two? If you don't want to, it's okay, but I need some."

"Sure, I thought you'd never ask. I always want to. A nice little puff would hit the spot right about now. I feel like my skin is trying to crawl off my body. There might be someone around who can help us out. Head for downtown. Lucas owes me a favour. If he can't help us out, I bet Andy can. Are you sure?"

Here we go again, Sam thought, with a mix of fear and excitement. This was exactly what started them down the road that led right to this whole mess. A tiny, almost inaudible voice screamed in his head. 'No, not now. Find Jane. Find Jane. You gotta stop.'

The thunder of his addiction drowned out the smaller, weaker voice of reason. It was almost easy to ignore. He couldn't help it. This other little voice that said, 'Don't worry, you can't do anything for Jane right now anyway. Get high, feel better. It won't matter. You'll stop feeling sick and you'll have a clearer head to find Jane.' That voice was a little louder than the first.

The second voice won. It wasn't even close. "Yeah, I'm sure. No doubt at all."

Sam was worried about Jane, but he was gonna snap if he didn't find a little treat. He would not go on a burn. His phone was on, he would answer it soon as they called him with Jane's location.

He couldn't keep going like this. He felt sick to his stomach and he couldn't think straight. Two puffs and a few hours sleep and he'd be much more help to Jane than he was now. Now all he was doing was walking and talking and not processing things. This was what he needed to help him focus.

He would save Jane. He had to. If he didn't, he knew he wouldn't survive. He would take too much of something one night and end it all.

He almost wanted to do that now and let everything float away forever. But he couldn't do it. He loved her too much. He wasn't that big of a coward; he couldn't forget about Jane. All he needed was a little taste to help hang onto his sanity.

His mouth watered at the thought and he pushed a little harder on the gas pedal.

22: Waiting alone

Lynda hated waiting. Patience had never been one of her strong suits. She would rather go to the dentist and have something drilled than wait around for anything.

She paced around the tiny room. There wasn't much space, so she walked up and down the small aisle between the two beds. Once in a while, for a change, she made a trip to the bathroom. It was even smaller, she couldn't turn around without bumping something. This place felt like a sardine can. It made her claustrophobic, but anything was better than sitting in a chair waiting. She expected Sam at any time.

Lynda had told the cop all that she knew. John had said she had done the right thing by coming to the police. He said to help Jane they needed evidence. They needed proof. They had to get everything on tape. Sam was going to have to wear a wire to prove what had happened to Jane, who was behind it and to stop it from happening again. She hoped they could talk Sam into it.

Lynda looked over at John, where he sat in the shadows by the window. He was a tall man, well over 6 feet. When they were both standing, she had to look way up to see his eyes. He had beautiful sad blue eyes; they were the first thing she noticed about him when they met. John was staring out into the parking lot for any sign of Sam.

Lynda was worried sick about Jane. Still, she couldn't help but wonder what it would be like to run her fingers through his hair. It was a little long for a cop, there was enough to tangle her fingers in.

She shook her head; this wasn't like her at all, checking out a man she just met. She must be lonelier than she thought.

It had been a long time since Jeremy died. After losing him to PTSD, she had promised herself she would never love another. She couldn't take the heartbreak of losing anyone else. First she lost her parents. Then her Jeremy. Jane was all she had left. She couldn't lose again. Lynda couldn't live with herself if she lost Jane, too.

John was smart and strong, but Lynda wondered if he could save her sister. Or was this going to turn into a bloody shitshow of legendary proportions?

Adam's old car pulled into the parking lot. She was so happy to see them arrive she didn't notice the black car that drove past the motel.

23: Touch someone

Sam woke up sitting behind the wheel of the car. Adam was sleeping, slumped against the window, drooling on his already dirty shirt. The LED on his Z30 blinked at him like a tiny bloodshot eye.

He grabbed the phone. Shit! Multiple missed calls and texts, a bunch of messages waiting.

They had gotten some nice rocks from Lucas. They had got really happy, really fast. Then they must have crashed hard. They couldn't have been sleeping that long, but it was long enough to miss that very important call. He fucked up. As usual. He groaned. What the fuck was wrong with him?

He scrolled through the list of calls. Lynda called. Calls from a number he didn't recognize. He opened a text from the unknown number. There were no words, just a blank message with a photo attached. He clicked the attachment and an image of Jane tied up and blindfolded with blood on her face filled the screen.

His heart sank. He punched the steering wheel. A small beep sounded from the horn. Adam never even budged.

Sam's hands shook as he pushed the button for voice mail, the robot voice said, "You have three new messages." The first was from Lynda. "Where are you guys? Have you found Jane yet? Meet me back at the motel." Next was a hang-up.

The third message was the one that made the hair on

the back of his neck stand on end. The one call he shouldn't have missed. He could hear Jane crying for help and the sounds of her being hurt. She screamed. Then a man's voice came on the line. The few words Sam heard over the pounding of his own heart kept chasing themselves around in his head. "Pretty soon she won't be making any more noise. You know what we want. Get us our stuff now. Or else."

He started the car in a wild panic and headed straight for the Rainbow. Adam mumbled something but didn't open his eyes

Sam was in such a state he didn't even notice the dark sedan that followed him. He had to talk to Lynda. They were going to need help to find Jane. A lot of help. There wasn't much time.

He took a left onto the old #1 highway. It would be the fastest way to get to the motel. The car with tinted windows turned left, too, and then disappeared down a side road and Sam still never noticed.

For the first time in months there was nothing else to worry about. Only Jane. Not where he was gonna get his next treat, not where the rent, groceries or gas would come from. His mind's eye was full of Jane. Beautiful, sweet Jane. His ears still rang with the echoes of her screams. It didn't matter anymore that she left him. That was his fault anyway. He didn't make her leave, but he sure didn't try to stop her when she left. He let her go. Tough guy, pretended he didn't care. Now, look what happened. He didn't take care of her.

The whole thing was all his fault. He had been a shit head. He had to find Jane, had to save her, even if she didn't love him anymore.

24: Patience

Sam parked the car at the Rainbow Motel. The parking lot was empty. It was the off season, and this wasn't a five-star hotel. That was mostly why he asked Lynda to meet him here. Sam thought it was the perfect spot to lie low.

He looked around the place; there was no one in view. There didn't seem to be anyone watching him. He pushed on Adam's shoulder until he woke up. "C'mon, pal. We got to do this."

"Do what?" Adam murmured.

Sam reached past him to open the passenger-side door and shoved him again. Adam chose to stand up rather than land on his nose.

Sam got out on his side and slammed the door behind him. He waited until he heard Adam's door close, then crossed the parking lot and knocked on the door of room 16.

Lynda opened the door, drew him inside and started to close the door behind him. Adam had his foot in the door, and Sam hauled him in.

Lynda closed the door and turned to him, ignoring Adam. "Sam, I had to go to the police. We need help. This is detective John Tower. He will help us get Jane back."

Sam looked at the guy in the corner, then focused on Lynda, "You were right to go to the cops Lynnie. I am scared to death for Jane. If we don't get the drugs back, these guys are gonna kill her. Listen to the message I got.

They texted a photo of Jane, too."

Sam pressed play and Lynda was in tears in seconds. Sam felt sick to his stomach.

Adam's face didn't change. Sam wondered if Adam cared about Jane at all or if he wanted to save his own ass. Sam wasn't that surprised when the cop asked them to wear a wire and Adam refused. He was a selfish piece of shit. He'd rather let Jane get killed than take any risk himself. It was Sam and Adam's fault Jane had been taken. Sam couldn't leave anyone in a situation like that, especially Jane. He didn't care if Adam wouldn't take responsibility, he would, it was his fault. Sam would wear the wire; he would do anything for Jane.

Sam listened to John's plan. "The first thing we need you to do is contact them, say you have the drugs and you want to meet them and make an exchange. The drugs for the girl."

Sam said, "I told you. We don't have the drugs! I wish to fuck we knew who does have them."

"We don't have time to find them, so we are going to have to fake it."

"That idea is gonna get us all killed," Sam said. "You are a cop, don't you have some drugs somewhere we can use to get Jane back?"

"Look."the detective said, "I'm not the one who decided to deal heroin and start this whole train wreck. There is no magic stockpile of drugs at the station that we can trade for your girlfriend. You are going to have to trust me and do what I say if we have any chance at all to save Jane."

"Fine," Sam said. What else could he say? It was the only option he had.

He sent the text, and immediately his phone buzzed. The tiny light started to blink signalling he had a reply. All that was on the screen was an address: *16037 Rockridge Street.*

Rockridge Street seemed familiar to him although he hadn't heard the name in a while. Then it came to him. "I know where that is. I used to work at a fish plant, cutting roe in the summers when I was a teenager. They closed it years ago. It's been empty except seagulls and rats ever since."

"Sounds like a good place to hide a hostage. Or set up an ambush." John said. "I'm sorry, Sam. This isn't looking too good for Jane, or us."

"I know, but Jane is waiting. Where is this gizmo you want me to wear?"

25: Turning wheels

Sam and Adam left the hotel and headed for the old fish plant. It was by the ocean, close to an hour away down secondary roads, so he had plenty of time to think.

Adam took another nap. If Adam couldn't be high, he would sleep. That was how he coped with life. Sam didn't care. Whatever worked for him. Sam had never been big on sleep, waste of time.

The sun had already set, and the sky was darkening. Sam drove as usual. Even though it was Adam's car, he didn't drive it; he had no driver's license. Adam lost it for impaired driving and no insurance a few years ago and never got it back. Big fines to pay first. He didn't do good at tests and the stress of a driving exam was too much for Adam.

Sam didn't mind at all; he enjoyed driving. He was good at it, too. Adam sucked at it, like he did most things, no matter if he was drunk, stoned or sober.

The radio played a steady string of classic heavy metal. Motorhead, Iron Maiden, Metallica. The music made him smile. He even sang along. A few words here and there. He figured if Lemmy's growl or Bruce Dickenson's scream were the last music he heard, he would be okay with that.

Detective Tower was going to be listening close by in his car. Sam hoped he would be very close by, and that he'd have a lot of backup if things went wrong. He had a bad feeling about this whole deal. If Thomas found out they tried to lie to him about the heroin, they would all be dead. If he found out he was wearing a wire, they were all dead. He was afraid that, no matter which way he turned, the reaper was waiting around the next corner.

Sam wished he knew what had happened to the goddamn bag of heroin. The centre of everything and all he had was a black hole in his memory. He remembered going to the club, but that was about it. Who else had been there? Had someone been watching him? Who could have known what was in the bag? He had no clue.

They had been more than half snapped when they arrived at the club. They were at least half gone everywhere they went. They were always giggling and acting like a couple of teenagers. Goofing around, everything was a joke. This was so far from a joke that he wasn't sure if he'd ever laugh again.

It didn't take long to reach full-blown blackout at the club. Sam had been in a bad mood since Jane left, so he dove headfirst into the whisky bottle and hit the pipe extra hard. He drank, smoked and stumbled along, behind Adam.

He didn't even remember the other girl that Adam said came home with them that night. She was a complete blank, except for the scent of her perfume, Cool Water, that's what she had called it. He loved the smell. It had been so strong he could still smell it. The smell connected to a happy feeling; it made him want to smile. They must have had some fun, even if he couldn't remember it.

That night, he had been looking for complete sensory overload. He needed to block out the reality that he had driven away the only woman he had ever loved. Drugs, booze, smokes, loud music, tits. It had worked. He had blocked out everything that was bothering him for a few hours, but Jane was the one paying for it. Her screams of pain and confusion were something he knew couldn't block out. No matter how much he drank or smoked. He had to rescue her. He had to bring her home.

Adam had done the exact same drop twice before on his own, so Sam had trusted him to do most of the work. Sam thought he'd tag along. Do the driving. He should have known better.

Adam never ever did any work. He always found a way to have someone else do it for him. Sam didn't know why he hadn't seen through Adam's shit sooner. He was a user, a selfish bastard, plain and simple. If you called Adam out on anything, he pulled the "My Dad ran out on me. Mum coped with booze, pills and a string of never-ending 'uncles'. So lay off, man" routine

Sam felt bad for Adam. His childhood was shit, no doubt about it. Sam thought no matter what, there came a time when you had to stop blaming other people for your life. You had to grow up and take control. Create the life you want. Be with the people who make you a better person. Sam had forgotten that for a while and got pulled into Adam's nightmare life. Now his own life was a nightmare.

This was not how he had pictured his life with Jane. She was amazing. Kind, caring and a knockout, with her dirty-blonde hair and ice-blue eyes. She had everything any man or woman could want.

It was the crack. He had been putting it before Jane, and she left him because of it. He hoped things would go right tonight, and they got Jane out of there. Even if she didn't forgive him, as long as she was alive. He could live with that.

Lynda would wait for one of them to call her. She blamed him for all this. She was right; it was his fault. Guilt by association.

Jane hadn't even known he was working for Thomas. She knew nothing about the drugs or the drop. He had never even thought it could affect her. He had thought it would be all over and Jane would never even know about it. Wrong, again.

Lynda would pace the floor as usual. She was always nervous and anxious. She smoked pot like a chimney to combat her anxiety and headaches. Sam doubted there was any amount of grass that would calm her down today. He hoped to be calling her with Jane safe by his side in another hour.

26: Waiting

Lynda wasn't waiting at the shitty hotel. She parked her car a couple of streets away from the old fish plant. She'd been here for a little while and had seen no cars go by at all. It was a deserted, lonely sort of place. Perfect for mischief.

She smoked a joint, tried to meditate and calm down. The way she felt right now, one joint wasn't going to cut it.

Like she could sit on her ass and wait at the hotel. As if she trusted Sam to save Jane. Lynda knew Adam was worse than useless. Jane was almost better off without their help. Fuckin' losers. She hoped John was where he was supposed to be. Sam would need his help. Hell, who was she kidding? John would need help himself.

How did she and Jane get into this mess? Lynda bartended and waitressed for a living; work was usually as exciting as it got for her. It was a quiet restaurant/bar. They had a few regulars. An older crowd. A dance every month. The most business was guys stopping for a cold one or a quick double on the way home from work. The only time voices got raised was if there was an argument over the last piece of pie, who was up next at the pool table, or if someone put too much money in the VLTs.

When she wasn't at the bar working, she was in her garden and greenhouse. This whole thing was way outside her comfort zone. She could not believe this was happening. It had to be a nightmare, not reality, Jane being kidnapped was so surreal. It had to be happening to someone else, that she had fallen asleep watching a movie or reading.

Why hadn't Jane told her things weren't going well with Sam? Jane always told her everything...at least, she used to. Ever since she was a little brat with pigtails in her strawberry-blonde hair. She told Lynda her dreams, her favourite things, even when she had her first crush on a boy. His name had been Alan. Back in the days when a boy pinched you or pulled your ponytail to get your attention.

Adam and Jane hadn't been together for much more than seven months. Anytime Lynda saw them they seemed totally in love. He opened her door; he pulled out her chair; they were always smiling and cuddling. At least when there were people around. Jane had always gushed about Sam. Maybe things were different when no one else was there. She knew all about that from living with Jeremy.

As she thought about it more she realized she hadn't been seeing them as much as usual, the last little while. They used to stop by, raid her little fridge and do laundry at least once a week. Those visits had gotten shorter and less frequent. Especially over the last couple of weeks. She should have known something was wrong.

She had been trying to give Jane some space and not hang over her shoulder all the time. This was the first boyfriend Jane had lived with, so Lynda was trying to let them figure things out on their own. There were always ups and downs, they had to learn how to deal. She would stay back and keep out of things if she could, but if Jane needed her she was here waiting.

She might even try to peek into the old fish plant. She needed to see Jane; she needed to know Jane was still alive.

27: Orders

Thomas sat across the big hardwood desk from Lewis. "They finally made contact. They will meet us at the plant with the package tonight. I had a guy tailing them: they are at a that hotel in the south end."

"It's about fucking time. This should never have happened. This is all on you, Tom. You've been in the game for a long time. You know how things work."

Lew poured himself a double shot of expensive whisky. "Keep a better eye on these things." He didn't offer Thomas anything. He wasn't company, he was an employee. Lewis emptied his glass and poured another drink. Then lit a big fat cigar and puffed up a cloud of fragrant smoke around him.

"You are right, boss. I'm sorry. I had used Adam before and everything was fine. He does what I tell him. I don't know what was different this time."

"'I'm sorry'? You look like a fucking sympathy card. 'I'm sorry' don't pay the bills." Lewis puffed several times on the cigar, and the cloud of smoke in the room thickened. "You can't trust a fuckin' junkie, you can trust two of them even less. I thought you were smart. Send Jim and Bobby to meet them, but don't take the girl. Keep her hidden at the cabin."

He poured another shot. "She is an ace in the hole, a little insurance in case these little shits try to fuck with us."

"After we get the package, then what?" Thomas said. It had been years since he quit smoking, but he wanted one now worse than the day after he quit. The craving would pass. It always did. He ignored it and focused his full attention on the boss.

"Do I have to spell it out for you?" Lewis slammed the glass back on the desk so hard, Thomas expected it to shatter.

Lewis sat back in his chair and puffed his big cigar. He gestured in a vague direction in the air. "Tie up all the loose ends however you want. Make sure they stay tied up forever. I never want to talk about any of these pieces of garbage again."

"Okay, I'll tell Bobby to handle everything. I'll tell him to close the books on this deal. Good chance for him to step up and prove his loyalty. No one will miss a bunch of crackheads. The next thing you hear about this is that it is all taken care of. Then we will be back to business as usual, boss."

"It better be, or else I'll start looking for a new right-hand man."

"Don't worry Lew, I have it all under control."

It might be time for the old man to retire. Thomas didn't like to be threatened. Threats didn't scare Thomas; they made him angry. If Lewis thought he could intimidate him he was wrong, very wrong indeed. Thomas demanded respect from everyone. Lewis seemed to have forgotten that.

He'd wait for the right time. Then he would be boss. Bobby was new; he would want to fall in with the new boss. Thomas was sure he could get him to help when the time came. He had a feeling it would happen sooner than later.

He'd heard rumours of the old man getting soft, even before this mess. Thomas had to take control before some eager "entrepreneurs" swooped in to claim it all.

28: Fish plant

Bobby and Jim were at the fish plant, waiting for Adam and Sam to arrive. Bobby was getting tired of this whole mess. He would be glad to be rid of those two burnout morons. The girl Jim could have. He didn't care. She was less than nothing to him.

All he wanted was the bag of heroin. That would make Lewis happy, maybe earn Bobby some extra cash as a bonus. Say what you want about Lew but he did take good care of his employees. If he was happy, everybody around him was happy. If Lew wasn't happy, it was best to stay as far away as possible. Breathing too loud when Lewis was mad was enough to get a guy killed and dumped in a ditch or swamp.

They should be here by now. He wondered if crackheads were ever on time.

Jim was hiding in a different part of the building keeping an eye out for any unexpected company. They had kept everything pretty quiet so they weren't really expecting anyone else to crash the party. Those two little shits would be too scared and stupid to go get help. Too bad for them, they were gonna desperately need it.

Next time he hoped that Thomas found more dependable delivery boys. He'd much rather be doing other things than fixing Thomas' mistakes. Junkies just didn't seem to be smart enough to even be able to drop off a package. How fuckin' hard was that? If you want something done right you had to do it yourself. He wouldn't hire a junkie to walk a dog.

Bobby saw a set of headlights slowly approaching the warehouse. It must be Sam and Adam. Looked like they were alone. No one following them.

His phone buzzed, a message from Jim. "Looks like the shitheads are almost here. You ready?"

He wrote back "kk". He was ready.

Bobby took a deep breath and took out his gun. He checked the clip and put a round into the chamber.

He watched Sam and Adam park, turn off the lights and get out of the car. They went around to the trunk and took out a black bag.

This wasn't going to take long. He would be home in time for supper. There would be time to stop at the strip club for a lap dance and some extra special treatment in the VIP room, before he went home to eat a home-cooked meal and bang his hot wife.

Bobby smiled. He did love the perks that came along with the job. If he cleaned this mess up properly, he might even move up in the business. The boss was going to notice him. He was tired of being the rookie. He was ready to take control.

The rusty, dirty door of the building opened and Sam walked in, with Adam following as usual. They both looked scared shitless. Both of them almost jumped out of their skin when the wind blew the old door shut behind them.

Bobby grinned. This was going to be easy and fun. "It's about time you got here. You are late."

"Yeah, I've been hearing that a lot lately," Sam said. "Let's get down to business. Where the fuck is Jane? I want my girl."

"Have a little patience, Sammy. You will see her soon. First things first. You tell me, where in the fuck is the heroin? That is what this meeting is all about, isn't it?"

29: Choices

John parked beside a dumpster by an old garage close to the fish plant. Sam needed to get out of there with the girl before the kidnappers figured out the bag didn't contain heroin. Sam had expected more backup, but only John was coming.

The chances of the exchange going as planned were low, pretty much nil.

Jane needed them. There was no other way. He shouldn't be working on this case as a drug case at all. The Captain wanted him to help clear the backlog of all cases, not just the drug squad cases. Everything from domestic violence, rape, break and enter, stolen cars to trespassing. They needed more officers, but it wasn't in the budget.

But John couldn't let it go. He needed hard evidence. Eyewitness testimony, with confirmation on the tapes. Then the department would have to back him up. Without it, he would have to keep quiet.

John waited for the exchange between Sam and the kidnappers. He smoked cigarettes and thought about Lynda. She looked like a nice lady. She adored her sister and had no family. Her long brown hair had looked soft enough to touch. An intriguing little woman, with a beautiful smile, but he already had one ex wife who hated him.

The job took up all his time. Even when off-duty he still thought about work. A complete workaholic. So much to do all the time. So many people needed help. The reason why he had joined the force. To help. The lowlifes and criminals never seemed to rest. The police couldn't afford to rest either.

John didn't wish being a cop's wife on anyone. Took a special kind of strong to handle being a cop's partner, or any first responders' spouse. Most weren't up to it. He tried to blame the job, but deep down he knew it was his own fault his marriage didn't last. Pam drank a lot. By the end of the marriage, she was having random one-night stands. She didn't hide it. Pam flaunted it, especially when she drank, and she drank all the time. She needed to be loved by someone, anyone, even a stranger.

John had ignored it. He ignored her. John paid no attention to life outside his main focus: the job. He didn't know his own kids, and Pam had gotten tired of doing everything alone. Her new husband was some kind of computer nerd who worked from home.

He didn't miss her at all, but he did miss being with the children. They didn't want to see him anymore, and he didn't blame them at all.

John checked his watch. Sam and Adam should be getting to the plant soon. He turned the earpiece on and waited to hear Sam give the signal that they were entering the building.

30: Dark places

Lynda crawled through the long, dead grass outside the old plant, trying to find a window to peek in. The building was long and didn't have many windows, with a taller part at the end, almost like a turret. She wondered what that weird spot was for. Sam and Adam were already inside; their empty crappy car waited by the building.

Half-rotten plywood covered the first window. She crawled along to the next broken window. Through a tiny crack in the plywood, she saw Sam, Adam, and a man she had never seen before. No Jane.

She ducked down and thought about what to do. She would have felt a lot better with John by her side. He would never have let her come here. If John caught her sneaking around, it would piss him off. Oh well, it didn't matter. It was too late to turn back. Him being pissed was the last of her worries.

She tried more windows. Maybe Jane was in a different part of the building. When she ran out of windows on this side of the building, she looked around but didn't see or hear anything out of the ordinary. Other than the wind, it was quiet. She was sure there wasn't anyone else out here.

Lynda ducked down and ran to the corner of the fish plant to look for windows in the back or a door where she could get inside. She didn't trust Sam to get Jane out, and she didn't know where John was. Lynda could get in and sneak Jane out while the boys were all busy.

Lynda continued in the dark along the back of the old building. About halfway across she found the outline of an old door. They had boarded it up at some point. Looked like whoever did it, did a shitty job. Most of the boards had given up and fallen off, or been broken by explorers of abandoned places.

She grabbed the last board and it disintegrated in her hands. She pulled the door open a bit and peered inside. It was so rusty it didn't even squeak, it just made a gritty scraping noise.

It was even darker inside than it was outside. Lynda didn't care. In her head she could still hear her little sister crying. Jane didn't even know anything about the drugs the guys were selling. Lynda would not wait for Jane to get hurt worse, or even killed.

She opened the door wider, trying to see in the inky blackness. As she entered the doorway a bright light blinded her. A man's voice said, "Don't move, bitch!" The voice seemed to come from all directions.

Lynda tried to back out the door and run, but something heavy hit her head. The last thing she heard was a man saying, "Well, well, what have we here?" He laughed.

She recognized that laugh, and it made her blood run cold. That was the voice she had heard on the phone, the guy hurting Jane.

Lynda passed out.

31: Stuck

Jane wiggled around in her chair. She tried to rock back and forth. The chair wobbled but wouldn't fall over. She had to get out of here, wherever 'here' was.

Jane wished she could get the blindfold off her eyes. She had never imagined covering her eyes could bother her so much. The ropes dug deep at her wrists and ankles, and they hurt something terrible. The gag was horrible; it made her want to choke and vomit. Still, not being able to see was worse than either of them.

In the darkness, every sound made her jump. A tree branch had scraped the window awhile ago and she screamed, thinking it was her captors returning. She didn't know how long it had been since the men left.

Jane was terrified and had lost her sense of time in the unwanted darkness. She shuddered to think what would happen if Jim came back. She couldn't defend herself and didn't have a chance against these guys. What had Sam done to get her involved in all of this? Where the fuck was Sam?

This entire mess was connected to Adam. Jane and Sam had been much happier before Sam started hanging out with Adam. Since then, Sam had started fucking up at work. He would be late, or not even show up at all. All the jobs started out okay, but that usually only lasted about two or three days. Sam would find a way to get fired, or he would quit and say everyone who worked there was an asshole. Then he'd get drunk and high with Adam and watch cartoons all day. She had hoped it was a phase, but it had been going on for months.

Finally, she had told Sam she needed a break while he decided when he wanted from her. She wasn't just going to cook and clean and take care of him. She wasn't his mother. He wasn't a baby. He had a baby of his own that he wasn't taking care of. Mikey was only two years old. Sam hadn't seen him in months. He owed his ex a lot of back child support and didn't want to give her any money. Said she'd spend it on crack. Denise said he was lying. That he was using crack. They fought back and forth. As long as Sam had no income, he couldn't give Denise a dime. He said he'd take care of Mikey himself. He wasn't giving in to Denise.

It was a childish game they played that drove Jane crazy. Is that how Sam wanted to live? Always fighting, screaming, drama, and drugs. Jane knew she didn't.

At first Sam was amazing, but after the first couple of months he started to change. He hardly slept. He started introducing her to new friends. She was thankful she never saw most of them again.

Jane went along with everything. She tried partying and hanging at the club with Sam, Adam and Trisha. She wanted to make their relationship work. If he wanted a partner, she was game.

If all he wanted was a waitress/housekeeper he was on his own. She loved him but she loved herself more. If he wanted to be together they had to be a team. He was 26 years old, for fuck sakes. He had to grow up. If Sam couldn't deal with her needing to be equal, then he could find a new girlfriend.

Jane strained against the ropes. She couldn't budge them at all. The knots felt like an expert had tied them.

They sure didn't want her to get away. Jane kept trying to rock her chair enough to knock it over. She wouldn't give up. Maybe if she tipped it, she could squirm her foot out of the ropes. It didn't sound like much, but it would be a start.

Even in a situation as crazy as this, Jane was still a glass-half-full kinda girl.

32: Words

John listened to Sam and Bob. Calm, making small talk. So far, so good. Just two guys having a chat. He hoped Bob didn't examine the bag. He'd have to wait and see. John had called in a favour from a friend at the department who worked the evidence room who owed him. Big time. He'd helped their daughter out of a jam once, and still, what he needed crossed the line. He didn't put it into too many words but the guy on duty took a bathroom break and John didn't sign the log book. No one would know where it went, if anyone noticed anything had even disappeared. Shit like this happened all the time, and not for as noble a reason.

Not far from here a department had lost hundreds of drug exhibits. The officer in charge said it's most likely they were mislabelled or misplaced. They kept better records for a couple months. That's as far as it went. They just made a few excuses and went on their way.

His plan was to do the same. He took a little heroin from the evidence locker. He was on his own if he got caught. He hoped that if Bob tested it, he would test the real heroin on top, not the fake bricks at the bottom. A long shot. If they were lucky and Bob was in too much of a hurry, they might squeak by.

He texted Lynda. "Should have some news soon, the guys are meeting now."

He moved closer to the abandoned fish plant in case

the guys needed him. No help to them sitting in his car. He left the equipment recording, but kept his earpiece in so he could listen to things unfold.

He stayed hidden in the darkest places as he made his way toward the huge, decrepit building. His black and grey clothes helped him slip by in the shadows.

The abandoned processing plant was long and skinny, with a shed of some sort at the end. He wondered why Lynda hadn't answered his text yet. She was quick to answer most of the time. Maybe she went to the bathroom. He was sure Lynda wasn't the kind of person to take her phone to the dirty bathroom with her. She seemed neater than that.

Before he could ponder it any further, he heard Sam, Adam and Bob talking louder and louder. It didn't take long until they were arguing. All at the top of their lungs.

John ran. For Jane's sake, he hoped he made it to them in time. This shit wasn't for softies.

33: Delivery

Sweat trickled down the back of Sam's neck. It soaked his shirt. He was so nervous, he couldn't help it. He wiped the sweat out of his eyes as he passed the big bag to Bob.

Bob grabbed the bag, hauled out a brick, and slit the package open. He licked the blade of the knife.

Then Bob smiled at him and said,"You are lucky you brought back our bag. Lewis will be glad you finally co-operated. He was very disappointed that the two of you had such a hard time to complete such an easy task."

Adam stood there silent. Looking at the ground. Sam didn't think Adam knew how serious this situation was. He'd be paying more attention if it had been Trisha they had taken instead of Jane. If Adam loved anyone, it was Trish. One thing for sure. Adam loved Adam most of all. Sam might need to make some new friends after this was all over, if he made it through tonight.

Sam wanted to say it wasn't his fault someone stole the package. Taking the blame was hard. He never admitted he was wrong, never. This was a first.

Instead, he said as mildly as he could, "I know we fucked the deal up bad. It means nothing to you, but we are so sorry. We wanted none of this to happen. It's all our fault. Where is Jane? Please, please let her go. You have what you want. Tell Lewis she has nothing to do with this."

"Have some patience, Sam. You will all be together

again soon enough," Bob said.

"Don't give me crap like that, Bobby. I want to see her now. Where is Jane?"

Sam wasn't nervous anymore. He was mad. "She's not here, is she? Is she even still alive?"

Bob opened a pack of smokes, took one out, and lit it. Sam noticed his hand didn't shake one bit. Steady as a stone. He figured if he tried to light a smoke, he'd have to chase it around with the lighter all day.

Sam said, "I'll ask again, a little louder in case you didn't hear me. Where the fuck is Jane?"

Bob took a deep drag on his cigarette, exhaled and said, "Jane is fine."

"She'd better be. She didn't look fine in the pictures you sent us."

"That? That was nothing. A taste of what will happen if you don't cooperate. My buddy Jim really likes her."

"He'd better not touch her," by now Sam was yelling.

Bob laughed. "Funny shithead, like you could do anything, anyway."

Bob edged towards the shadows. Sam glanced at Adam. He stood, slack-jawed in a daze as usual. He could have been standing in a park staring at the sun. The big battery-powered light that was sitting on a wobbly old table flickered. Bob walked over and hit it. It stopped flickering and shone bright again.

A door at the back of the long room crashed open and bounced off the wall. Jim stomped through it, dragging behind him a half limp Lynda with blood in her brown hair.

Sam had thought it couldn't get any worse. He was wrong. Again. Fuck, he couldn't believe this was happening. It felt like he had to be having a nightmare, or watching some fucked up movie. First Jane and now Lynda.

Sam was frozen with shock. Before he could react, the light went out. It was pitch black inside the warehouse, and he could no longer see anyone.

He didn't know where Adam went when the lights went out. He had been watching Bob. In the darkness.

To his left he heard Bob yell, "Who the fuck is that, Jim?"

"I don't know who she is or what she is doing here, but I caught her snooping around out back. So I decided to bring her along," Jim yelled back.

Sam knew he had to get rid of Jim and Bob fast if Lynda, Jane, or any of them would survive the night. He took out the gun. He had never even held a gun before tonight, let alone fire one. He hoped it was as easy as they made it look on TV.

34: Into the darkness

Adam dove to the right when the lights went out. There was a heap of cracked plastic tote boxes and broken pallets that he might hide behind. He crouched behind the broken boards and boxes, listening hard to guess out where Sam, Bob, and Jim were. He had had a feeling something would go wrong. That was the way things happened to him: constantly going wrong.

Usually, he blamed someone else, but this time he had no one else to blame. He took this job and pulled Sam and his family into it. Lewis wouldn't let their fuck-up slide. No way out if Lew didn't want to let them out.

Adam was stupid, but he wasn't a fool. If Jane wasn't here, she was probably dead already and they all would be soon.

He struggled to see. He crawled in the direction where Sam might be. Adam wished he had got his hands on a gun, too.

He heard Lynda struggling with Jim in the dark. Adam yelled, "Let her go!" and started crawling towards the sound of the struggle.

They shuffled around in the black with muffled grunts from Lynda and swearing from Jim.

He didn't go far when an arm wrapped around his chest and another hand covered his mouth. The outline of the grimy white trim on his jacket let him recognize it was Sam.

Lynda fought back hard. That didn't surprise Adam, she was a firecracker. Good for her.

If Lynda got away on her own, they could concentrate on finding Jane. Every second counted. Always something crazy going on in his life, but this one took the cake. He couldn't imagine what Sam was going through. If it had been Trisha instead of Jane, Adam didn't think he'd be in as good shape as Sam. Adam would fall apart without Trisha. He wanted to help Lynda and Jane.

He whispered in Sam's ear, "Keep your head down. We gotta get the girls. Give me the gun."

35: Hit and miss

Bob headed for the steel table with the flashlight on it. He hit one bent leg and sent the whole table skidding sideways. The flashlight tumbled end over end, crashing to the cement floor. *Fuck!*

He jiggled the wires and tried the light again. Nothing, the light was toast. He'd use his phone, it had a bright light.

Jim grunted somewhere in the dark, then it was quiet again except for the wind howling around the broken windows and scattered junk all over the plant.

Bob threw the light hard out into the darkness, hoping to hit one of the two morons. Long shot but possible. He listened, hoping for a cry of pain to give away their hiding spot, but the light just bounced off the concrete.

When he found them he was going to shoot them both and set the place on fire, then go to the cabin to do the same. Shoot Jane and burn the place down. It would all be taken care of. No evidence, no witnesses, no proof, no crime.

Besides, he liked fire. A lot. More than anything. Almost more than pussy. Fire made him happy and he could never get enough. Well maybe not more than pussy, but right up there at the top of the list.

Bob yelled, "Hey, Jimmy, you got a handle on that chick or what?" No answer. "Jim, ya playin' or what? Where the fuck did you go?"

All that answered him was the howling wind. *Great. Fuck. Now what?* This whole thing kept getting better and better. There were four other people in this building, and he couldn't hear them. God-damned storm. It never rained all fuckin' summer, but tonight it seemed even Mother Nature was against him, personally.

He would be patient. Eventually one of them would move, breathe, fart or sneeze. Bobby would shoot first and ask questions later. Screw it, he'd shoot now *and* later.

He fired a few rounds into the dark, but nobody moved. He'd flush them out another way.

Bob kept backing up as slow as he could until his back hit the wall. He moved slowly along it to the left until he found himself beside a pile of old broken pallets and flattened boxes. Looked like some kids had planned a fire and hadn't lit it yet. He'd help them out. Get the party started.

Bob took out his lighter and held it against some strips of cardboard until they caught. Watched the flame sputter and almost die, then flicker and grow stronger. That should get them out of their hiding spots a little faster. He wished he'd grabbed his supplies from the trunk. He'd have had a big fire fast. He had things more flammable than paper, things that would burn even in the rain. Then he would have had them hopping fast.

Following his dancing shadow he headed to the back of the building to see what the hell Jim was doing.

36: Rescue

John ducked in through the broken door at the back of the fish plant. There hadn't been any fish here for years but he was sure he could still smell them. At least the wind wasn't blowing in his face anymore.

He thought he smelled a whiff of smoke, stronger than the old fish smell. He hoped it was just his imagination.

Outside beside the ocean, it was deafening. Inside it was a little quieter, but the wind was howling around the old building like a banshee. The sea was crashing at the breakwater and throwing up seaweed and rocks. The rain would probably start soon.

John was worried about Lynda. He had found her car parked close to the plant. Inside it, he found her keys, purse and phone but no Lynda. He hoped she hadn't run into Bob or Jim. He should have known better than to expect her to stay at the motel alone.

He waited by the door for a few extra minutes, but he didn't see or hear anything. He took him time and made his way along the wall trying to find another door. He finally found an opening; again he waited and listened.

A bright light cut through the darkness and bounced around the room. It blinded him for a second. John shielded his eyes as he crouched down trying to stay hidden. The light started moving in his direction. Out of nowhere, a shot rang out. It was loud in the warehouse. A woman screamed. The flashlight stopped moving and clattered to the ground, pointing at nothing. He was sure the scream had come from Lynda.

A man's voice came from the far end of the room. "Where are you, Sammy? Adam? Nosy mystery woman, are you still here? Come out, come out wherever you are." Then laughter.

John knew the voice, it was Bob. He needed to find Lynda and get her out of here. Then he could help Sam and Adam.

As John crawled towards where he thought the scream had come from, he could still faintly hear Bob taunting Sam and Adam. If they stayed quiet, he would never find them in the vast darkness of the old fish plant. John wished he had some backup. For once he thought having a partner might be nice.

Then John heard a groan to his left. He found Lynda! He whispered in her ear. "Shhh, It's me, John. I'm going to get you out of here."

"Oh John, I don't think Jane is here. I didn't see her. I tried to look for her. I couldn't find her."

"Even if she isn't here, Sam and Adam are. We have to try to save them and find out where Lewis is hiding Jane. I'll tell Bob and Jim the only way to stay out of jail is they have to testify. The judge will go easier on them if they lead us to Jane. We have to try."

Two more gunshots echoed through the plant. Then screams—sounded like at least a couple of people were wounded...or worse.

"I have to get you out of here. You shouldn't be here," John said. He helped Lynda crawl to, and out, the same door they came in.

Once outside in the rain. John could see that Lynda was pretty much okay, except for the gash and bump on the side of her head. That was going to need some stitches. "That's a pretty nasty cut, but you'll live."

He tried not to smile at Lynda, and was still a little pissed she showed up, but couldn't stop himself. "You shouldn't be here at all."

"I couldn't just sit and wait. I was going to go crazy in that little room." She touched her head and winced. "I'm not sure what he hit me with, but it fuckin' hurts."

"Go get in your car and get out of here. Go to the hospital and get that taken care of. You can't help Jane if you are dead."

"I don't want to go leave you and the guys," Lynda said.

"I'm going back in to get them right now. I need to know you will be far away.""Fine. I will go to the hospital. Please call me the second you know where Jane is. Be careful. Bring my sister home."

"I will," John answered. He hoped he could keep that promise.

He hugged her and said, "Now get your ass out of here."

John headed back inside the creaky old building. On the way in, he scooped up the flashlight Lynda had dropped. It was working. He turned the light back off for now; he didn't want to be an easy target.

The smell of burnt gunpowder hung thick in the air, but he hadn't heard any more shots. Maybe they were all dead.

John knew who the boss was now. No matter how tonight ended, he would go after Lewis. John was sure the department would back him now that he had this whole thing recorded. He had lost the earpiece but Sam's mic would still send out audio. Plenty of evidence. He would ask the prosecutor to offer Sam and Adam immunity if they testified against Lewis.

37: Reaching

Lynda was here, and Jim had caught her. It was not something Sam expected to have to deal with. He was still trying so hard to figure out what to do next. He never even thought twice when Adam asked him for the gun. He just passed it over.

When Bobby shot at Lynda, Adam fired a few shots in the direction of the muzzle flash. One shot must have struck home because Bobby screamed. Then all was quiet again after the deafening roar of the handguns.

Sam whispered, "You okay, Adam?"

"Yeah."

"You hit him."

"He hurt Lynda."

"I hope not. Maybe he scared her, and she's hiding. Let's head for the back, where we last saw her."

"How are we gonna find Jane?" Adam whispered.

"I don't know. We're going to have to see if Bobby or the other guy is alive enough to tell us where she is. If not, we are going to have to talk to Thomas."

Sam half crouched, half ran across the room towards the back door of the plant, avoiding the deep drain holes the length of the floor that used to be covered by metal covers, long gone and sold as scrap metal. Adam stayed close behind.

There was no sign of Lynda, but about 30 feet away from the door, Sam tripped over something. He felt around the cold cement. It wasn't a drain. It was a man's body.

Lynda hadn't just fought back; she had killed him. He had been impaled on an old piece of rebar sticking out of the crumbling dividing wall.

Good. Sam didn't feel bad at all, only relief. Jim had to be the piece of shit that had been beating Jane. He kicked the body. Hard, twice. He wished he could kill him again.

He wondered where Lynda had gone. She had to be hiding. He wasn't that far from the door. Did she get out or did she hide in another part of the building? There must be empty offices, bath rooms, or supply closet that she could be hiding in.

Dim yellow light came from a street light on a telephone pole halfway across the parking lot. Sam could see the outline of the door. He hoped she got out.

He wondered if Bob was alive. "Hey, Bobby how the fuck are ya? You still alive, you fucking lying asshole?" Sam yelled. His voice almost echoed off the far wall of the big room but was swallowed by the deafening roar of the wind.

No answer. Good. Sam hoped Adam had killed him.

"We can get out of here now. We have to go see Thomas and get him to give us back Jane." Sam said. "We're wasting time."

"You can't reason with Thomas," Adam said.

"Well, we have to do something. Every minute we wait is another minute Jane is in trouble. Thanks for taking the gun when I froze, Adam. If it wasn't for you we'd both be dead."

"If it wasn't for me, we'd never have been here at all," Adam answered.

Even with the wind roaring like an unseen giant outside, Sam heard a loud click in the deep darkness.

"Well ain't this sweet?" Bob said from the shadows. "If you two are done sucking each other off then we can end this shit."

"Fuck you, Bobby. Where are you hiding Jane?" Sam said.

"No, fuck yo—" Before Bobby could finish his sentence a bullet whizzed by his head and he dove back into the blacker shadows for cover.

"Run, Adam!" Sam yelled.

"This way Sam! It's me, John. I'll try to cover you. Move, move!"

"And they say there's never a cop around when you need one." It relieved Sam to hear John's voice, but he couldn't relax yet. They still hadn't a clue where to find Jane.

They ran for the door. If they could get outside, they could pin down Bob. Sam hoped Bob was wounded. If they could get his gun away, then they could make him tell where Jane was.

38: Matter of pride

Thomas looked away from the dancer on the stage and glanced at his big-ass Rolex. It was 12:45. He should have heard from Jim or Bob by now.

He would wait a few more minutes, and then he'd give Jim a call. They better fucking answer their goddamn phones. This mess had been going on for long enough. It all ended tonight. He went back into his little office and closed the door. He felt so closed in, in that office too much, he often thought about knocking a wall down and making it bigger. He was a big man; it made no sense to jam him into a tiny box all night. Thomas should have a huge office with a private window to the stage. That would be one change he would make as soon as he was running things.

His phone buzzed from the top of the big polished hardwood desk. The big desk fit his large stature, but in the small room it seemed almost comical. Every time he moved around the office, he knocked over the trashcan or sent the paintings askew. He wasn't a clumsy man, but it looked like he was when he was in here.

He glanced down at the screen, expecting to see Jim's number, but no, it was Lewis. Great, the asshole he wanted to hear from. Having Lewis on his ass every two minutes would help no one.

He read the short text, pretty much what he expected: "Are we happy yet?" Thomas didn't bother to send an answer. He didn't have the answer Lew wanted. Better to keep quiet. When this was all wrapped up he would talk to Lewis, over a drink and a cigar and explain the whole thing. He didn't even smoke cigarettes or cigars, but he puffed on one of the big stinky Cubans politely when he was with Lewis. If Lewis was feeling generous enough to offer him one. It hadn't happened often. Thomas didn't mind, he wasn't big on male bonding. It would be rude to refuse the offer.

Until he knew the situation was under control. There was nothing new to say. Another angry text from Lewis: "You can be replaced. I can replace all of you." Lewis's threats were getting old fast. Texts were easy to ignore.

Lewis was like an old lion, his roar still sounded strong but the body and mind were beginning to fail. He kept ordering everyone around, and people were doing what he asked, but doing it slower all the time.

Thomas was getting tired of having to answer to a boss. He wasn't making enough to take shit from Lewis. It was about time for him to become his own boss. The girls here at the club liked having him as a manager, so he was sure they would like him even more as owner. No one would be sad to see "the hammer" gone. If any tears were shed they would be happy ones. A new lion was ready to take over the pride.

He texted Jim. "What the fuck is going on? Lew is getting impatient."

He also sent Bob a message to cover all the bases. Neither one answered him. Thomas called both of their phones, again, no answer.

Fuckin' peachy. He threw the phone back on the desk in exasperation; it slid across the polished mahogany. He was sure it would slip off the edge and crash to the floor to land in a million pieces. He was so sure, he thought he saw it happen. Thomas didn't believe his own eyes when it stopped and hung on the edge of the desk.

He went through a lot of phones. What good was technology that didn't work right? If they didn't call in soon, he'd have to go to the plant and see what the hell was taking so long. It should be done by now. It looked like if he wanted this done right he would have to go do it himself.

He had to get out of this room. He would take a drive while he waited for the call. This shit town had a Water Street and a courthouse, but was too small to really even have a south end. The whole damn thing was south end.

That was half of why they ran their club here, almost an hour from where he lived. Wanted a small buffer between work and real life. Tom didn't need to see the dancers or bar patrons every time he went to the store for gas. Though the long drive got tiring sometimes. Like now, he needed a pick me up.

Thomas decided to pull over and walk around a bit to wake up. He hoped the fresh air would do him good, but he was too far from town to smell the ocean. He'd be able to smell it soon; he hated that smell at low tide. He wasn't a big fan of the manure he had to smell all the way here, either.

This place had two kinds, fishermen or farmers, and they all stank. They all liked to spend money at the club, though. That, at least, made Thomas happy.

39: Waiting

When Lynda got back to the car, she backed it farther behind the building so it was even more hidden than before. Anyone passing by shouldn't see her at all. With luck, she could tail someone to Jane.

She didn't know what else to do. She was all out of ideas. This wasn't something she ever thought she would ever go through. This had to work.

Lynda found a half-full container of Advil in her purse. She was so happy to see it, it almost glowed like it was the holy grail of headache pills. She swallowed three turquoise pills with water from a plastic bottle from under the seat. It was warm and tasted terrible after sitting in the car. Stale, and the plastic aftertaste was worse than the pills themselves would taste if she'd chewed them up.

The wind and rain felt good after the day's heat. It had been hot for weeks with hardly any rain all summer. She caught handfuls of rain and tried to wash the dried blood off her hands and face.

Lightning danced in the clouds on the other side of the river. She could feel the rumble of the thunder coming closer. The storm would be big when it hit. They were forecasting power outages, and storm surges along the coast. She hoped she would have found her sister before then.

She rolled herself another joint, smoked and wondered, *Where, oh, where is Jane, is she even still alive?*

Lynda couldn't believe it was possible Jane could die and she wouldn't feel something. She would know in her heart. They had always been closer than a fresh shave. A deep connection, more like twins than sisters. Spending whole days together without even speaking.

She wasn't surprised at all when she couldn't find Jane at the plant. Her presence wasn't something she could feel there at all. Jane had never been anywhere near it.

John had told her to go to the hospital and she had said she would. He should have known better. She told him what he wanted to hear. Lying to a cop might not be the best plan, and a cute cop at that, but Lynda wasn't going to the hospital. Not while Jane was still missing.

She was going to follow whoever left the abandoned fish plant and find her sister. She hoped it would be John, with the kidnapper locked in cuffs. A girl could dream.

The glow of headlights got brighter, coming from the direction of the old processing plant. Whoever it was, they were moving faster than a long-tailed cat in a room full of rocking chairs. Finally, she would find Jane.

She dry swallowed another couple pills to knock the pain roaring in her head down a few notches. The first three had done little. Her head hurt most of the time, anyway. Nothing new. She could live with it.

40: The way out

Adam was sure the storm was trying to tear the building down around him. Shit was blowing everywhere and there seemed to be a big piece of the roof trying to let go over his head. He almost wished it would all come crashing down and end this madness. Somewhere on the wind, he was sure he smelled a hint of smoke. It made him think of campfires he used to have when he was younger.

One of his mother's boyfriends had a little shack by the river. The adults usually kicked him outside in the first hour. Hell, in the first 5 minutes. His mother would say, "Go play outside, hon, you don't want to stay here and listen to grown ups talk about boring grown up stuff." He didn't think it sounded boring by the howls of laughter. Passion, and later the inevitable fighting and screaming a few minutes before dawn. Then quiet.

Even though Adam was only ten he didn't mind being alone. He was always glad to get out of there. It was safer and cleaner outside with the animals. Inside there were half-naked, snoring drunks all over the shack.

The fire was his babysitter. He found it funny: he hadn't thought of those long nights of watching the flickering fire turn the wood to ash in years. He found it was pretty sad that this was one of his best memories of his childhood.

Adam had almost forgotten about John until he heard him yell. It was the first time in his life he was happy to see a cop.

"Let's go." Adam looked at Sam. He could tell how scared and worried to death he was for Jane. "You go first, I'll cover you. Then John can cover me. "

"All right, man. Keep your head down, and thanks for having my back," Sam said.

"I'll always have your back, bro. You are my best friend, Sam. Now let's go."

Adam watched Sam like a hawk watching a rabbit as he started to scurry across the cold concrete floor. He fired a couple of shots into the darkness in the direction he had last seen Bobby. When he looked back at the door, Sam was outside the building.

Good: one down, one to go. Not to mention Jane was still missing, but they had to save themselves first, then they would save her.

"Come on Adam," John yelled. "I've got you covered. You have to hurry up, come now!"

The howling wind swallowed his loud voice, the way the ocean swallowed a sinking ship. One second there, the next gone without a trace.

"I'm on my way."

Adam stayed crouched down as he crossed the floor heading towards the door to freedom and Sam. The hardest thing he had to do in his entire life was to take that first step. When he didn't get shot after a second, he took another step and another. He was only twenty feet from safety. It might as well have been two hundred feet, or two thousand. The path to the open doorway stretched before him like an eternity.

He fired a couple more shots into the darkness over his shoulder. No one shot back at him. He thought maybe Bobby was dead, but he wasn't sure. John fired a few cover shots into the warehouse behind him.

Adam kept moving, half crawling. He was now down to 10 feet. There were a few more feet of cracked cement between him and the relative safety outside.

He was almost there when the first bullet tore into his leg, close to his hip.

Adam screamed, stumbled and fell to the floor. He managed a couple of words. "Run, Sam, get outta here."

Adam guessed that Bobby wasn't dead. He had been playing possum. The last thing he saw as he fell was Sam screaming "No!"

The second bullet made a small, neat entry hole in the back of Adam's head. The exit wound in the front was a different story. His face was torn off in an explosion of brain tissue, blood, bone bits and broken teeth. He never had a chance.

41: Running

Sam watched as Adam first stumbled and then fell to the floor. Bobby heard a scream from outside as he pulled the trigger a second time. The bullet tore most of Adam's head off. *Good*. His time at the gun range had paid off. He'd never have to look at his skinny junkie face again. All this shit was Adam's fault, anyway.

One less thing to worry about. His to do list was getting shorter.

He didn't know what he was going to do about Sam. And who the fuck was this John, and the woman that had been with Jim? He had been sure these two losers would have no backup at all. He had been wrong. Jim would have called that a rookie mistake.

Since he hadn't heard a peep from Jim since that choked-off scream, he figured Jim wasn't calling anybody anything anymore. That didn't bother Bobby at all. In fact, he was more than a little glad Jim was out of the picture.

All he cared about was getting the heroin back to the boss and cleaning up this mess. Fuck Jim, if he'd been doing his job right he'd still be here. He had more than one ex-wife but no kids, so there was no one to mourn him anyways. Jim had truly been an asshole. He wasn't one of them guys who weren't so bad once you got to know him; he only got worse the longer you spent with him. The irony of him being taken out by a woman was priceless.

Bobby crawled backwards away from the door Sam

had just gone through. At least he got one of them; small comfort in that thought since now there were at least three more people he had to find and silence, plus the girl at the cabin.

He would be busy tonight. Places to go, people to see. He had to think about this, had to make a new, better plan.

First thing, he knew they had at least one gun, 'cause one of them had shot him in the arm, it was a shallow flesh wound and he would live, but it fuckin' hurt like a son of a whore.

He knew another way out of here. The old emergency exit door on the other side of the building led right to where he had hidden his car. Planning his exit when he went in, he had thought he might need to make a quick getaway.

On his way outside, he noticed the little fire he lit had gone out. Guess it wasn't as dry in here as he thought. *Fuck*. He should have used more than paper to get it going. He had no excuse other than pride; he thought there would be no surprises, that he had everyone pegged. He figured he would just shoot them and have lots of time left over for cleaning.

He didn't have time to stop and relight it now. He had brought everything he needed with him; it was still in the trunk. He just didn't have time to get it, he had to get out of here and talk to the boss. Tonight was not going according to the plan in any sense of the word.

He grabbed the bag of heroin and ran outside to his car. He had to call Thomas and find out how he wanted to fix this mess.

He got in the car and looked around. He didn't see anyone; maybe they thought he was still inside. He didn't start the car or turn on the headlights, thinking it would be a good idea to coast for a while before starting the engine.

Wrong again. A bullet smashed the driver's-side window and lodged itself somewhere in the backseat. So much for not being noticed.

Bobby started the car and gunned the gas. The car slid sideways in the mud, but Bobby was a pretty good driver and kept control.

That had been his old job, wheel man. Now, not very many years later, he wanted to make more money, get more respect, be feared. Once he took care of the situation, he should be moving ahead nicely. It was a mess but maybe he could use it to his advantage. No one would ever fuck with him if they saw what happened to Sam and Adam and whoever else got in his way.

He steered the car out of the skid and sped away as fast as he could. He was lucky the tires were new on this car.

He saw a pair of headlights following him from the fish plant. He pushed a little harder on the gas to try and stay ahead of them.

Once he hit the pavement Bobby dialed Thomas' number, hit speaker phone, and threw the phone on the seat.

"Where the fuck are you? It's about fucking time you call and check in," was how Thomas answered. No time for small talk. He wasn't big on small talk ever; he only wanted to talk about bigger things, like the state of the country, where to travel or what to invest in.

"I'm just leaving the fish plant. Everything is fucked." Bobby said.

"What the fuck are you talking about? I thought you two could handle a couple of crackheads and a skinny little girl." By now Thomas was yelling, not trying to quiet his huge voice at all.

"I got the bag. That's good, isn't it, boss?"

"At least you got one thing right. You want a gold star? What else?"

"I think Jim is dead. Haven't seen or heard tell of him in quite a while. Last I saw of him, he was dragging a petite brunette behind him, and she was fighting pretty hard. That little fucker Adam is dead, too, I know that for sure. I watched his skull shatter when I shot him in the head."

"What about the other one, Sam?" Thomas asked.

"I'm sorry, boss, he got away from me. He had someone helping him. I'm ninety eight percent sure he was a pig. He smelled like a fuckin' cop. It caught me off guard."

"You were supposed to clean this up and leave no evidence. Now you're telling me there are more people involved, including fucking cops? Did you at least get rid of the building, hide your tracks?"

"No, the fire went out. I had to get out of there. They were shooting at me, I took a hit, I shot Adam and I ran. I need backup, boss, we have to shut this down tonight. "

Another bullet flew by. It missed him by half an inch, but a rain of sparkling shards and splinters of glass landed in his dark hair. He swerved, stomped the gas pedal, as if it could go past the floorboards. He put his good arm out the window, and fired a couples shot at them without looking back.

"Fuck, they are right on my ass, Tommy! I don't know how long I can keep this up. I'm going to end up putting the car in the ditch if I don't slow down soon. What do I do? Where should I go?"

At first, Thomas didn't answer, lost in thought, or maybe he just didn't know what to say. The line was so quiet, for so long. He didn't even hear him breathing. Bob had a crazy thought that he'd hung up.

"Tommy! Thomas! You still there?"

"Yeah, I'm here. Lead them out of town to the cabin. Give me a few minutes. It's almost closing time anyways. They don't need me here to lock up. I'll meet you there and we will finally put an end to all of this."

"Okay. Sounds good to me."

"Keep your head down Bob."

"That's the plan, boss, that is the plan."

42: Old dog

No one was telling Lewis anything. He had a bad feeling about all the shit that was going on. No one was answering his calls or texts, and that meant only one thing. Shit was out of control. He didn't like it when things weren't in control. Lewis' OCD wouldn't let him leave shit out of order.

He doubted Thomas. He didn't seem to be able to do his job anymore. Thomas had been Lewis' right hand for years, but lately he didn't seem to be as sharp as usual. Hell, maybe he was having a midlife crisis. Maybe the job was getting to him. Lewis had seen tougher men crack. It happened.

It was high time to take control, time for the boss to get shit done. He had been feeling a little old and grey and more than a little useless lately. This would fix that. Dye fixed the grey hair, that helped some, but the real confidence booster was power. Nothing like shooting someone to boost your confidence. Committing murder always made him feel superior to weaker, lesser men.

He double-checked his gun to make sure it was loaded. One in the chamber, the clip was full, and he had extra clips in his pockets. Usually he let the hired help do this kind of thing, but sometimes a man has to step up and prove himself. He would show them once and for all that no one fucked with Lewis or his shit. No matter how old he got, he still ran this town. He was on top of the pile and planned to stay that way.

He sent a text to Thomas. and to Bob for good measure. Both said the exact same thing. Short and to the point. He didn't fuck around.

"I'm on my way. This better be fixed by the time I get there or I'll fix it myself."

He didn't expect any answers. He hadn't got any word for any of them in hours. Fucking shitty cell service around here. No towers for miles; they were years behind the times. Took forever to get a signal sometimes, and then when you did the call dropped. Fucking technology, supposed to make life easier.

He knew exactly where the cabin was. He should: it was his. Paid for with cold hard cash he made from selling sex, drugs and sometimes death. He had bought it years ago when one of his mistresses wanted a quiet getaway. She was loud in bed but shy outside the bedroom, so the cabin was a perfect place for a quick loud frolic in the sheets. With no close neighbours, she went wild. She had actually lasted quite a while, a couple of years if he recalled correctly.

Reminiscing made him smile. Eventually, she cracked and ended up in rehab for booze and coke. She'd needed a lot of it to put up with his bullshit. He was not an easy man to keep happy.

He paid for it all. Lewis took care of his mistresses. He didn't mind most of the time; he could afford it, and the tail was worth it.

Lewis missed that one a little. Her name was Tanya or Terrie or something like that. He didn't remember the last time he'd been up to the cabin with her.

It wouldn't take him too long to get there. It wasn't that far, forty or fifty kilometres. Especially when he was driving—he had a lead foot, even at the best of times. Patience was not one of his virtues. If he had any virtues.

He was going up there to get the heroin and shoot the rest. This would be the last day he felt out of control. When the sun rose he would be greeting the new day with a smile on his face.

He ignored the barely visible shake of his hand as he grabbed the steering wheel and started the engine.

Lewis knew his fancy smoky silver caddy wasn't made for back roads, so he took his big truck. It was an even darker grey, had huge tires and a good strong winch on the front. The ruts wouldn't stop him from getting to the cabin. Nothing would. He loved his big truck. It was his baby. He had no children.

That was a good thing. He hated kids, and he hated his ex-wives. He couldn't be bothered with people under eighteen years old. They didn't have any brains. It took experience to get smarts. If you didn't have any by the time you were eighteen, you were screwed no matter what lifestyle you led.

Going mudding was one of his favourite pastimes, even though he never had the time to do it often. Tonight would be fun. Murder and mud.

He revved the big engine and laughed. It had been a while since he felt so alive. It was like going hunting. He had sat in the shadows on the sidelines too long. He would take care of his business.

This was going to be a night to remember.

43: Tired

The club was still packed to the rafters even though last round had already been called. Trisha should be back soon to help close up. Denise had had enough for the night. She wanted to go get Mikey nice and early, so she was leaving as soon as she could.

It was an extra-rowdy crowd; they were extra-cheap, too. The bouncers were earning their money tonight. She had seen them throw out many overzealous patrons, and one of them was a woman. Thought she could get up and dance on stage with the strippers. Even tried to take off her own clothes. She looked good, too.

The girls didn't like free tits on their stage; they were trying to get paid. She was outside on her drunk ass before she knew what had happened.

Denise couldn't wait for her shift to be over. The night kept dragging on. She worried about Mikey. Trisha wasn't back yet. It shouldn't have taken her very long. Hope she found Mikey's meds.

Fuck it, she would skip the VIP room tonight. Like most people, she always needed the money, but tonight the money would not be enough.

She didn't even bother to change into clothes, just threw a jean jacket over the lacy robe she wore and ran to her car. As she left the parking lot, she again called Amie's cell. No answer. She hoped Amie and the baby were sleeping, and that she was all worked up first nothing.

A few minutes later, Amie called back. "Sorry I didn't answer, Auntie, I was giving Mikey his medicine. It seems to be helping already. I'm glad Trisha was able to bring it over."

"Me too, hon. Trisha is a doll. Since he's settling down, I guess I can stop at home for a quick shower and change. Then I'll be right over."

"Sure, we're fine. No hurry," Amie said, trying to stifle a yawn. "He's almost asleep already, and me, right along with him!" She laughed a very exhausted laugh and hung up.

Denise walked up the driveway in her bare feet, dangling her sparkling high heels from her left hand. She thought, *I'm so lucky to have some great friends in my life.*

She'd half worried she might have to break into her own house to shower, but when she tried the knob, the door opened. Denise let out a sigh of relief. That was one less thing to worry about.

Inside, she dropped her purse and shoes, and let the few clothes she was wearing slip off her body and fall to the hardwood floor. She was so tired; it had been a long night, damn a shower would feel so good. She wished she could take a long hot soak in the tub, but no time for that tonight.

All she wanted was to go over to her sister's to cuddle with Mikey. That was all she ever wanted to do: be with her little man. But she had to feed him and keep a roof over his head, on her own since his Dad was no help at all. Useless was a good word for him.

Denise appeared to float naked down the hall to the bathroom like a sexy spectre in the dark. Light from the yard light she had forgotten to turn off shone in the curtainless window, illuminating parts of her as she moved, mostly from the knees up and the shoulders down.

She took her time. She had no energy to rush even if she wanted to. Trisha had left no lights on inside at all. No matter, she knew the way to the shower by feel. She was one of those people who never slept well and made what felt like a hundred trips to the bathroom a night. She rarely turned on the light, so as not to wake Mikey, who was sleeping in her bed most nights. Or right next to it in a portable playpen.

The house was large enough that he had his own room and crib, but she liked having him as close to her as possible. Where she could reach out to touch his warmth and feel him breathe. To know he was okay. As he grew older there would be plenty of time to sleep in his own room in a big boy race car bed; she was already saving up for it.

44: Hot and wet

Denise took a deep breath and closed the bathroom door behind her, walked over and turned on the hot water full blast and let the room begin to fill with steam. She loved her bathroom. It was her sanctuary. It was one of the reasons she had picked this house. She fell in love with the bathroom.

It was like her own private spa, with a huge bathtub with relaxing jets and an amazing steam shower. Heated tile floors for her toes and a towel warmer for fuzzy warmth when she finally got out of the water.

Some people bought a house for the kitchen; not her. Kitchens and cooking didn't mean shit to Denise. She lived on coffee and cigarettes. She hadn't learned to cook much of anything yet. Her mother had been a terrible cook and apparently had passed that skill along to her daughter. So far she could handle warming up bottles of milk, making mooshy cereal and mashing bananas, but she knew soon enough Mikey would want a little more to eat; he was cutting teeth already. He was growing so fast.

A small part of her wished he could see more of his father. Boy, could he cook. But Sam didn't want to see them, she and Mikey were *personae non grata*; he had left them to fend for themselves.

Fend they did. Denise worked hard to make enough money for her and baby Mike to not starve, and she took nursing courses on the side. She spent a lot of time in the champagne room, but she did it all for Mike. Work was work, flipping burgers, office work, shovelling shit or dancing. If you really thought about it, any job you did made you a whore, and the only difference was how well you got paid.

Someday, she could stop dancing and work in a hospital or doctor's office helping people. For now, she did what she had to, to help keep a roof over their heads and food on the table.

She still couldn't believe Sam had left them. She thought he loved her and that he worshipped Mikey, but it seemed his habits topped the list of priorities and he would rather spend his time and money on that. She hoped he enjoyed it; he didn't have a clue what he was missing with his son.

Well, once she got rid of that bag in the closet she could leave all this behind and really have a future, somewhere without Sam, the club or anyone else. Just her and Mikey. Somewhere warm. Somewhere to feel free. Somewhere they could grow.

She might even call Thomas tonight. Well, it was really this morning. She was sure he wouldn't mind getting woken up for something as important as the bag.

Then there was Sara. That was a whole different mess. Since Sam had left her, Denise hadn't been with a man. Sure she danced for them, flirted for extra tips; but that was all. There were plenty of other girls who were willing, if a customer wanted more than she could give. She had thought about sleeping with every guy she met and throwing it in his face, but she had enough of manipulation and spite.

He had stayed alone, too, for a while, but that got lonely fast. He soon had a new girl. *Good for him.*

Denise had always been more than a little curious

about women. She was tired of being afraid. This was as good a time as any to give in to her desires and see what all the fuss was about. After all, she did work in a place full of beautiful, young, nearly-naked and, sometimes, completely-naked women. It didn't take her long to meet someone.

She had only known Sara for a couple of weeks, but she had never felt like this before. Sara was so beautiful...her eyes were mysterious and unreadable and her lips, they were so soft. Her perfume followed her like a sweet cloud that you could happily drown in. She wished that they were together, cuddled up in her big king-size bed, but she knew Sara had to work. Sarah had her own place and her own bills to pay.

No one knew they were together. It was their secret, a good secret. They just worked at the same place, as far as anyone there knew.

Technically, they weren't really an item. They had agreed they wanted to have an open relationship. No strings. Just fuck friends. Denise wasn't sure about it but just went along to see where this would go. She was usually a very jealous person, and she didn't think she could handle the open relationship thing. She was trying to change her life, but was this for the better? Choices, you never knew if they were right or wrong until it was too late.

She had to stop thinking about Sara, Sam, everyone, for just a few minutes. She was going to think herself crazy.

Denise tried to clear her mind. She took another deep breath and stepped into the steaming warmth. She took deep breaths in and out, counting each inhale and exhale. After a few minutes, she was almost in a trace. She swayed back and forth in the hot steamy water and washed the sweat and glitter of the club and its patrons off her body.

This was the best part of the night. This steamy heaven. Her body wash smelled like pretty purple lilacs, her favourite flower. The hot soapy water ran down her shoulders and back, it flowed off the curves of her breasts and hips like little shimmering waterfalls. With the help of the steam the scent of lilac was everywhere.

She loved the hottest water she could stand, and looked like a cooked lobster when she got out. She had to use gallons of moisturizer, but hot water was just so comfy. It felt good. The searing hot water felt alive. She even made her own shower lotion bars and sugar scrubs so her skin felt amazing despite the too-hot water.

Denise wanted to soak in the big tub with a giant lime bath bomb and some candles so bad, but she was sure she would just fall asleep and drown.

The water started to get a little colder, the hot water was already running out. That always made her sad. She shut off the faucets just before the water turned icy cold and grabbed a huge, warm, fuzzy towel and went to find some clothes to wear, maybe even some cozy pjs.

She thought she might have one lonely pair in the bottom of a drawer that she had been given as a Christmas gift and never used. She usually slept nude—much more relaxing not being all restricted wrapped in a layer of clothes plus layers of sheets and blankets—so she didn't have much of a selection of pajamas. Tonight she felt like flannel and a quilt. It was raining now and in the damp air she felt so chilled.

Lingerie, now: that was another story. She had a whole closet full of that frilly, see-through, lacy stuff. Usually they weren't comfy to wear. She wasn't bothering with that tonight.

She couldn't find any pjs so she settled for yoga pants

and an oversized t-shirt with a dolphin on it that was too ugly to wear in public. It had belonged to her big brother Joey from a vacation years ago. He was 6' 4" and no one made fun of him for wearing dolphin t-shirts. It was was too long for her, but he let her steal it anyway.

She wished he was here, but he lived a couple days' drive away and had his own little family to take care of.

45: Floating in the darkness

Never in her life had Jane been so thirsty. The relentless, burning thirst was the worst. The gag didn't help that feeling at all.

How long had it been? More than hours, she was sure. Days at least. Jane hoped they weren't planning on letting her starve to death. The hunger pains came and went, but the thirst was her constant companion, never for one second letting her forget she couldn't have a drink, not even a sip, and might never have another.

She tried to feel her fingers and toes. She couldn't feel them moving. She thought they were wiggling a little bit, but they were pretty much numb. Her arms and legs had also gone numb ages ago. Pulling and squirming as hard as she could had only seemed to tighten her bonds. It hurt.

Eventually, she had peed in the chair. It was so hard to do. There was no choice: her full bladder won. It had been easier after the first time.

Trying to figure out how long she was here was one way she tried to occupy her mind. It was hard to concentrate on anything in the quiet black.

Hunger, thirst, pain and fear. They all blurred together in endless darkness.

Fighting panic. It felt like a Mack truck was sitting on her chest. She knew the heavy feeling was anxiety from her sister describing it to her. If she hadn't known better she would have thought she was having heart troubles.

It had never bothered her so badly before she found out she was pregnant, but it seemed she had lots more to worry about now. At least she knew what it was, and that she wasn't having a heart attack.

Screaming against the gag for a while, more than didn't help, it made her feel even more sick and frustrated. She had never felt this way before. Completely hopeless, leaning towards madness. hoping for it all to end. Now she knew what it felt like to be an animal caught in a trap. If she made it through this she might become a vegetarian or even a vegan.

She hovered somewhere between asleep and awake, unsure how much time passed between. She tried to sleep as much as she could. That had always been her way of coping, sleep, hoping to dream. Then, by the time you wake up, whatever is going on bad in your life has passed.

Her teenage years were like every other teenager's, a confusing crisis all the time. Even for a boring nerdy girl with her nose stuck in a book. So she had spent plenty of hours sleeping her time and troubles away. But not like this, not tied up, alone, fearing how this would end.

She tried not to think of the baby. If she did, she panicked again. Normally thinking about the new baby would be a wondrous subject for a pregnant girl. But now it caused fear. What if she wasn't able to protect the baby?

No matter how many times she fell asleep, she kept waking up here in the same nightmare. Her sister would have snickered and called it groundhog day, but Jane didn't feel like laughing. Thinking of Lynda's usually dark sense of humour and her quick laugh made Jane want to cry more. She wanted her big sister. She wanted a hug.

Wasn't anyone going to come and get her?

Jane was so furious at Sam she could taste it. How could he get her into this? Somehow she left his broke ass and still got pulled into his drug problems. She didn't care if he was high, that wasn't the problem. She could understand why someone would enjoy it. Getting high, having a drink, relaxing, having fun were all good with her. It was the cost. It was the money and the lies.

She cared about the money he spent, the bills that didn't get paid, and dangerous situations like this. She had never in her wildest dreams imagined he'd get into this much trouble. She had thought some night he might get beat up, or at the worst arrested for possession. He had come home with a black eye and split lip before, but blamed it on him and Adam having a tiff.

She should have known the story was much longer than that. This was way worse than him getting busted.

She had wanted a little stability, a job, even a part-time one, a car that worked, the rent paid on time. Little things were all she wanted. Not the moon.

Now even the little things didn't matter. All she wanted was to keep breathing and get her ass out of this place. Talk about living in the now.

She heard an engine. It seemed to be getting closer. It wasn't very loud. It was the first sound that wasn't wind or rain that she had heard in hours.

She started in her chair. Her eyes fluttered open against the blindfold and she was wide awake. She tried to relax and pretend she was still asleep.

Jane was terrified. She felt like a mouse cornered by a barn cat, no way out. She wished someone had told her not to get involved with a crackhead. Oh yes, her friends did tell her, but she didn't listen. She was a big girl, she dated who she wanted.

Granted, she didn't know he used crack for the first few weeks of dating. Once she found out, she had already fallen for him. She should have stopped seeing Sam right then, as soon as she knew.

He was so sweet to her, when he wasn't making excuses or trying to scheme up some money. He kissed her on the forehead and made her feel like a queen.

It didn't matter now, any of it. She knew she wasn't a queen to cater to and spoil. Just a woman, who would soon become a mother. A single mother. That was if she made it out of this place. Or maybe all women were queens; she was getting a little loopy. She wanted to live, more than she ever had in her short life. For herself and the little spark of life that was growing inside her.

Jane slumped against the ropes and waited for the arrival of whoever now controlled her fate. She almost wished they would hurry up, or go away forever. The suspense was killing her. She was not a patient person; she was like her sister. Instead of wait and see, Jane'd be pacing, stomping and sighing like an old horse chomping at the bit. As if she had been waiting for ten years instead of a few minutes. Now minutes did feel like hours.

The sound of quiet footsteps came up the stairs and then stopped outside on the porch.

46: Going places

Sam and John ran the five longest minutes of their lives through the wet darkness to John's car. Once they were inside it, Sam punched the dashboard. He screamed and punched the ceiling. All he did was bloody his knuckles.

John let him vent for a while. After he tired himself out, John said a few words. He doubted they would help, but he felt like he had to say something. "Sam, I'm sorry about Adam. No one should have to watch someone they love die. You can mourn your friend later. Right now you need to get hold of yourself. I know you are freaking out about Adam, and you should be. Shows you aren't as stupid as you look. It's a huge problem. But we can't help that now. I'm sorry, but we still have to think about Jane."

"I know, I know," Sam sobbed.

John put the car in gear and got them going.

After a bit Sam wiped at his face with his blood-spattered jacket sleeve and said, "Step on it! Don't lose him or we are fucked. We need to find Jane."

John stared at the car ahead of them. "Shoot at him. Let him know we aren't giving up. If we can get him off the road, we can force him to take us to her."

"You are a cop ain't ya? Can't you call for backup?"

"I'm not supposed to be working on this case at all. The lieutenant told me to stay away. He or someone above him may have been paid off or scared off by Lew and his goons. This comes from way over my head. That's why I haven't called it in. I won't get any help. I'll get my ass handed to me and probably a suspension. We are on our own tonight."

"Great time to tell me now, I thought the cavalry would come. Don't the good guys always win? Don't you have any work friends at all?"

"Sorry, that's only in the movies. In real life, the good guys don't always win. Just ask Adam. No heroes are coming but us. No one else would risk their career on a case like this. Not for a grouchy old cop like me. Not for a junkie like you. They'd let it slide. They treat me the same as I treat them. If you haven't noticed, I'm not the friendliest guy. All I've been doing is trying to get to whoever is at the top. It's been a long climb. You guys happen to be my direct link to Lew."

Same gestured ahead. "Don't lose him, but pull back a little and follow him. Let him take us to Jane. It'd be better if we could keep our eye on him, so he can't ambush us. If we lose him now, we're fucked. Whatever happens to me after that, happens."

He glanced at John and said, "You seemed pretty friendly with Lynda. I saw the looks. You old dog, she was looking at you the same way when you weren't watching."

"What are you talking about? When?"

"At the hotel. She was staring at you from across the room."

"You are dreaming, crackhead," John said, like a grumpy old man.

Sam thought he saw a tiny smile pull at the corner of his lips. He hid it well, but for just a split-second, it was there. John must have noticed her looks, too. She looked a little too long to ignore.

One minute they were driving along, doing a good clip trying to catch Bob. The next they were spinning towards the ditch. "What the fuck, John, did you forget how to drive?"

When they crashed into the ditch, they weren't going very fast. John had slowed the car a little. At least the airbags didn't go off. They both already felt like shit, airbags in the face would not have improved the situation. The ditch wasn't deep, but they were stuck.

John turned off the ignition. "I can fucking drive. We blew a tire. With all the water on the road, I couldn't hold it. Are you okay? Anything broken?"

"Yeah, I'm all right. I had my seat belt on, like a good boy."

"Let's check out the damage, see if we can change the tire. I doubt we'd get a tow truck to come out here, wherever here is, even if we wanted to."

"Fuck, so much for us staying on his tail."

"Don't worry man, we will find them. They want us to. How else can they get what they want? When their trap is ready. We will be right where they want us. We have to be smart."

"First things first, I guess. I'll change the tire. Pop the trunk for me, will ya?"

John pushed the trunk release button while Sam went around to the back of the sedan. Too bad it was John's own private car and not a police cruiser. There would have been some weapons in the trunk. Instead all there was was a bald spare tire and a jack. He was hoping the spare wasn't flat. It wouldn't surprise him in the least. Murphy's law, and all that.

Sam could change a tire in no time. He used to spend his summers working at a garage. He enjoyed working on cars. He could have slapped a patch on it in a flash, too, if he had one. In the mud, it might take a couple of extra minutes but it wouldn't be long, and they would be back on the road looking for Jane.

The tire was buried in the mud. He might do a little swearing, but it would get done fast and right.

When he was tightening up the second lug nut, he saw headlights coming. He kept his head down, doing what he was doing; John could talk to them. Whoever the hell was out in the middle of nowhere at this time of night.

He was surprised when the driver's window opened, and he heard Lynda say, "Hey, you, need a ride?"

"Lynda! What the hell are you doing here? You should be at a hospital seeing a doctor!"

"I had a psychic flash and I knew you guys would need some help, so here I am. I'm the cavalry come to the rescue. Stop fucking with the wheel and get in here. That car is stuck. How were you going to get out of that mud hole, anyway? We have to find Jane. What's the plan? You do have a plan, right?"

"If you are psychic, sister, why don't you know what the plan is?"

"I'm not that good yet, sonny. I get a tiny tingle now and then." Lynda laughed.

Sam looked at her with half a grin. She had always had a strange sense of humour.

47: Hitchhikers

Lynda stopped when her headlights flashed off the window of a car in the ditch. She had hoped it wasn't John's car, but it was. At least it was them and not the kidnappers. That at least, was good luck, wasn't it? It was all about perspective. She hoped they were both okay.

When she got closer to the car she could see John: he was all in one piece. His hair was plastered to his face. He looked so young standing there in the rain, he looked almost innocent, not like a cop at all. That made her happy.

A soaked Sam was changing the flat tire. He looked okay, too. Well, he looked a little bit like a zombie, pale and gaunt, but he was alive.

"Need a ride?"

John ran around the passenger side of the car and jumped in. He leaned over and hugged Lynda tight. "You shouldn't be here," he said, while burying his wet face in her hair.

"Well I am, so deal with it." She squeezed him back.

"Yes, ma'am."

"Come on, Sam, let's go." She beeped the horn.

Sam got in the back seat, wiping the raindrops from his face and hair, his clothes were soaked. "Good thing the rain is letting off. I think I would have drowned standing up out there. Thanks for picking us up, Lynda. I didn't expect to see you for a few more hours."

"I couldn't wait for morning. I had to know what was going on. So sue me. So what do we do now? Should we call them or wait for their call?"

No sooner did she speak the words than Sam's cell phone rang. Only this time it wasn't Thomas calling. It was almost worse; it was Trisha. He wanted to hide.

"Fuck! What do I do? This is fucked. I can't talk to her now. Telling her Adam is dead...I just can't do that over the phone." His voice cracked at the thought. "I don't know if I can do it at all."

At first no one said anything. They just looked at the ringing, vibrating phone in Sam's hand. It had a picture of Adam smiling on the screen, with a happy Trisha kissing him on the cheek. It was too much.

John, forever the hard as nails cop, was the one who spoke. "Just ignore it for now. She will find out he's gone soon enough. It won't help anything to tell her right this second. We can worry about Trisha once we find Jane. Someone will tell her in person when the time comes. It won't have to be you."

Sam just sat there, looking more miserable than ever.

"We should call Thomas and see where he is," Lynda said. "Wherever it is, it will be an even bigger trap than the fish plant. John, can you call anyone? Won't anyone in the department help you?"

"Not a chance. I can't call anyone, I don't know who is on his payroll. All I know is I'm not. Hard to know who I could trust."

"Not one cop you can trust? Man, that must be quite the place to work."

"If I call this in now all that will happen is they will arrest you. Me too. I'll lose my badge. And the circle will continue. We have to do this right. We need lots of evidence or we need to put a bullet in all the bad guys."

"I'm for the bullets," Sam said. "These guys aren't going to let any of us live. It's us or them."

48: Taxi

This shit was real. John figured that Sam knew how real this was from watching Adam die, even if Lynda didn't. Even with her having to fight off Jim, she didn't seem to get it.

This was too dangerous for her. For anyone. Even cops. This was special-tactics-level shit. Not bumbling small-town police. It would be hard for a SWAT team, let alone a cop, a bartender and a crackhead.

It almost sounded like the beginning of a joke, but not a funny one. He didn't want to laugh, not even chuckle. If he wasn't involved he might have found the whole thing funny; cops had a weird sense of humour. Most of the time their jokes were dark, but that was the way they coped.

But when you were one of them, you knew that, deep down, they weren't laughing. They were fighting to hide their true feelings. Bury sadness, anger, even fear and happiness behind masks and crude remarks. Being a cop you had to be an actor, too. You needed a big mask.

They had already lost one of their small group of four; he hoped not to lose any others. He wished he had some backup. He had to help these people. Once this was over he would need a vacation, maybe even retire. Far, far away from the job and this town.

"Why don't you let me drive, Lynda? Your head must be killing you." He could see the huge lump on the back of her head peeking through the matted hair and blood. At least the bleeding seemed to have stopped.

"That sounds great, John. Try to keep this one on the road. There is no one to rescue us if you ditch it again."

"That was the tire's fault."

"Sure, sure whatever you say."

She kind of slid across the front seat and over his lap to reach the passenger side. It was faster than getting out in the rain and mud again. He was happy to see a little flush come to her cheeks when she mumbled a nervous "excuse me".

"I was glad I didn't meet any cars on the way here. The headlights would have made me crash. I guess he hit me harder than I thought."

"You should be at the hospital," John said. "You probably have a concussion. At least go get stitches and medication. You shouldn't be running around in the storm."

"Save your breath. I know everything you are going to say and I don't wanna hear it. I need to see my sister. I need to hold her and know she's okay. I will not sit in a hospital without her. I'll go crazy. They would have to tie me down and sedate me to keep me there. Headaches are nothing new to me. I can make it. I am medicated, always."

She glanced toward the back seat. "Sam, call Thomas and find out where he wants us to go."

"Wherever he has Jane, he will try to kill us. If Jane is even still alive."

"I believe she is still alive. I have to. If she was dead, I'd know it. I'd feel it. When you call, make him put her on the phone to show us she is alive."

"We can't trust these guys."

"Well, we can't wait for morning. Call Thomas."

49: Bad boys

Only a couple of his windows had small bullet holes in them, not that a smaller bullet would have killed him any less. That goddamn cop had been close, more than once. Bobby had been lucky. He must have had a couple horse-shoes stuck up his ass.

He couldn't believe he actually lost them in the maze of back roads on the way here. It was easier than he expected, after he shut off his lights for a sec. The rain helped too: the roads were extra shitty and the cop had hydro-planed into a ditch. At least the weather seemed to be on his side.

Bobby hoped they hit a fuckin' culvert. He drove around the wooded area for at least a half-hour after he lost them to be sure no one else was following him. They could come find him when he wanted them to, not before. He needed to get shit ready.

He pulled into the driveway of the little cabin. Bob made it around the big mud hole in the road leading to the driveway. It was a nice, private spot, with no neigh-bours for miles, a little bubbly river and lots of woods. Heaven.

He figured the girl inside might not feel the same way. Too bad for her. Not his problem.

He swatted at a mosquito that bit him on the back of his left hand as soon as he opened his door. Maybe it wasn't heaven, with all these flying fucking bloodsuckers everywhere.

He wondered again where the hell Thomas was. He figured Thomas would have beat him here. He had been pretty wound up on the phone. For fuck's sake, this was such a mess.

He should call Lewis. No, he figured it would be best if he and Thomas cleared all this up.

He brushed some broken windshield glass from his hair—man, they had been close. Those fuckin' crackheads had somehow gotten the jump on them. He should have known they would rat to the pigs. What was that saying about honour among thieves?

Oh well, at least he had the bag. That was all that mattered to him.

It was a nice cabin. Too bad it wouldn't see morning. Before he had a smoke, he figured he'd better take more time preparing things than he had earlier. He didn't want the evidence-cleansing fire to go out this time. He wanted it to burn hot and fast.

He opened the trunk and took out two small containers of fuel. One had kerosene and one had oil. This time he would do it right and destroy the evidence. Fire would hide pretty much anything. They would know it was arson, but arson was the last thing he worried about. By the time any firetrucks got here, it would be a pile of smoking rubble.

He stuffed kerosene-soaked rags into the wood piled against the back of the building. He soaked other rags in oil and did the same. There was an oil barrel that ran a furnace for those nights when you didn't want to bother using the cozy fireplace. Propane tanks for the bbq and kitchen stove.

He whistled a happy tune while he worked, like a crazy little birdie. Setting fires made him happy. He had always loved fire. Big inferno or tiny candle. It didn't matter if it was a tiny wooden match or a blazing crackling building; he loved it all, ever since he set his first one when he was only eight. He was a little kid but he knew fire burned. He loved playing with matches and lighters. People were careless. Everyone he knew smoked when he was a kid, so it was no trouble finding matches lying around. Fire was fascinating, almost hypnotizing. It pulled him in.

Once everything was set, Bobby rewarded himself with a smoke under the covered porch. He threw the mouldy, damp seat cushion onto the porch and sat his tired bones in the old wooden rocker. It was comfy for hardwood. It was in great shape for being outside; it didn't even squeak when he rocked. It was like being on vacation for a minute, long as he didn't think about inside the cabin or what would happen later.

He'd see the girl inside soon enough. She wouldn't mind waiting a bit longer. She didn't know how lucky she was to not be seeing Jim again. If he had a choice between a bullet or a few hours with Jim and then a bullet, he would pick the former.

He pulled out his pack of smokes, but instead of a cigarette, he lit a joint. A cigarette, even good ol' green death, his long-time favourite, just would not cut it right now. He felt around in his pocket and pulled out a small flask. He took a long pull of smooth whisky and slipped it back inside his dark jacket.

He could hear any cars coming long before they got to the cabin. The road was more than a little rough and you had to go slow. Even slower with the rain. The headlights would give them away before he'd be able to hear them. Lots of warning if the pigs found them.

He doubted they would, though. The cops around this town were slow and incompetent, and well paid to be that way. He himself usually hand-delivered the fat envelopes of cash to one of the older cops. So he was confident no one would bother him except the party-goers already invited.

By the time the cops arrived, it would be all over. Whether that was due to Lew greasing a few palms or pure lazy complacency of small-town cops, he wasn't at all sure.

He sent a text to Lewis: "At the cabin. Have the bag. Waiting for Thomas."

No answer. He didn't know if Lewis would bother to answer anyone as low on the ladder as him. He more often went through Thomas. Never direct. But he sent it anyway, to be safe. Covering all the bases. They left nothing to chance this time. Fucks ups were not getting pinned on him.

He sent a text to Thomas, too: "At the cabin. I have the bag. Hurry the fuck up."

Still no answer. Uggh. The storm must be fucking with the cell signals. Nothing new in this backwards ass town. "No Fucking Signal" should be the cell phone company's name. He should have heard something back from them within seconds. He knew they weren't fucking sleeping. Fuckheads were usually playing Candy Crush on their phones. Always had them in their hand, even when they went to take a shit.

As he was finishing the tasty Vanilla Kush, he heard a car. The engine was revving high. It came close to getting stuck a few times trying to navigate the water and mud that used to be a dirt road. Not exactly a road made for cars, or for drivers who couldn't handle themselves, at least not today. It was still a few minutes away.

He got up and ducked around the back of the cabin to wait and see if it was friend or foe. They had never installed security cameras. No one knew about this place or used it much. Cameras would have been a nice thing to have right now instead of waiting to see who came along.

When the headlight cut the darkness, he was glad to see it was Thomas' big car and not some hunter or lost camper. The way things had been going it wouldn't have surprised him much. Finally, they could get this deal done. He went back to his comfortable rocking chair.

Thomas walked up the driveway checking out Bobby's poor car. "She's fucked, Bob. I can see that by the windows. You're lucky you made it here without a few extra holes in yourself."

"I ended up with a new little hole, nothing I can't handle. A new scar to show the ladies. The kinda girls I like love scars. Too bad Jim wasn't lucky enough to make it back this time. Ah well, gives me an excuse to go car shopping next week. Maybe I'll look for something sporty. How do we deal with this situation, anyway?"

50: Cabin in the woods

Thomas rounded the last corner on the road to the cabin. It was rough even at the best of times. Lew never came here anymore, so the road had fallen into disrepair. No dressed-up ladies in low-slung sporty cars had been back here to see Lew for awhile. The property had just been sitting back here, quietly rotting away.

Fuckin' ruts. He could feel the car bottoming out. He hoped the damn thing didn't get stuck; that would just top everything off.

He made it through the last big puddle, more like a pond. He thought he should have brought a boat. It would be all over soon enough, though. They would call the losers and tell them to come get their girl. When they arrived, he would shoot them. End of story.

He parked beside Bobby's car. Looked like Bobby would need a new one. Thomas could help him out with that when they got this all finished. He would deserve a bright, shiny new ride if the rest of this went according to plan and ended here, now, with no witnesses and no evidence.

That bag of heroin was worth more than a car. Two lives had already been paid for it and there would be more blood spilled before they were done. He didn't give a shit about the little nobodies who would not make it home tonight. They had made their own beds. He was just upset that this whole thing had made him push up his plans for taking over the business.

He knew that Lew had been to the doctor a lot lately. There was something going on. He had heard whispers of the big C. Lewis smoked those big, badass cigars, and there was always a stinking cloud around him. Tom wouldn't be surprised if it was his lungs. He was coughing more and more.

Thomas had hoped nature would do him in all on its own. Now he knew he couldn't wait that long. He wanted to take his time but couldn't; he had to act now. Lewis was pissed, and this time there was no telling who would come out on top. If Bobby backed him up tonight, maybe he would be the right choice for Tom's old job when Lewis was out of the picture and Thomas was in.

When the wind blew towards him, he could smell kerosene before he got within twenty feet of the cabin. He knew how much Bobby loved fire. Truly loved it. He had once paid off a security guard to lose some surveillance footage that showed a burning building that Bobby was standing across the street from, watching the flames climb all over the building like it was a giant drive-in movie screen. Bob had been first on the scene, so naturally the suspicion, if not the blame, immediately landed on him. Thomas spent some of his own money to make it all go away.

Bobby owed him, big time. He had kept the tape for himself. It was locked away in a safe place. Not Lewis nor anyone else knew nothing about it. You never knew when something like that would come in handy.

He told Bobby to be sure he was never caught anywhere near the scene of a fire, whether he set it or not. He would have to enjoy the flames from afar or if, it was a big enough fire, in the newspapers and local news. If Bob got picked up at the scene of fire again, Thomas would let him rot in jail. No second chance.

Being a criminal was easy. Being a successful criminal was another story. Most didn't learn from their mistakes and kept making them over and over again. Thomas was smarter than that.

The boys in blue had picked up Thomas just once, when he was only 14, hardly old enough to shave. He'd just been a stupid kid. He had busted a bunch of windows at a girl's house who had turned him down when he asked her for a date. She could have just said no, but she laughed when she said it. Laughed in his face. As if she didn't act different when they were alone. She liked him well enough then.

He had just walked away, face burning and tears stinging, but he had never forgotten that lost, hurt feeling of being laughed at by someone you wanted to love you. She and her girlfriends and their boyfriends had a great laugh.

He wasn't laughing when he busted every goddamned window in her parents' house, but he was smiling. Until he got picked up in a squad car and brought to the cop shop; then he wasn't smiling at all.

After a night inside a cell, he swore he'd never go back there. Jail taught him some life lessons fast.

He had learned a lesson about trust, too. Some people would tell you anything you want to hear, when they want something from you, then laugh at you like you were a clown when they have what they want, or someone to show off for. He made sure to never put himself in a position where he anybody could make a fool of him so easily. Never again would he feel the hurt of being used for another's gain or amusement.

Thomas had learned fast. He never saw the inside of a jail cell again. He tried to teach that lesson to those around him. One chance was all you got with Thomas.

He kept the same attitude in all aspects of his life. The club, the gym, and in his bed. Most women never saw his bed more than once, if he brought them home at all. If he did, he saw something in the way they carried themselves that he liked. Not just their beauty, although any brunette with hazel eyes would draw his hot attention. They had to be smart, strong, and small and sexy, and they had to know when to keep their mouth shut and do what he said, when he said to do it.

That wasn't a combination he found often. Even though he had a huge appetite for sex, he lived alone.

He would purposefully abstain for days, sometimes weeks, at a time and focus only on his muscles and getting bigger. When he couldn't stand himself anymore, he'd drive a few hours to the real city and throw around some money. If he was in the mood, maybe he'd pick up a couple of dancers at a club.

The chicks who flocked to his table he only laughed and joked with. While he partied he watched the waitresses and bartenders. They were more his type, hardworking and modest.

He was a sweet talker when he wanted to be. He could make his rough voice into a soft rumble and had a smile to make any woman melt. He cut a dashing figure in his suit; it was cut to emphasize his bulging muscles, wide shoulders, and small waist. He made the expensive, tailored clothes he wore look good.

He was a hit with the ladies, for a while at least. Once they got to know him, none of the women stayed around too long. High-maintenance wasn't even the word for it. He didn't blame them. He wasn't a bucket of sunshine, even on a good day.

When he saw Bob in the circle of the yellow porch

light, rocking back and forth in the wooden rocker, smoking a joint like it was a lazy Sunday afternoon, he grinned, Bob sure was one cool cat. Even when they were shooting at him he had stayed calm, kept himself alive and the car on the road, while he talked to Thomas the whole time. Hands-free my ass, that took nerves of steel and being able to concentrate on more than one thing at a time. He had what Thomas needed. Great big balls. Today he would have his fire.

Thomas stopped for a second by the shot-up car and spoke up to Bob from the ground for a while in his regular gravely voice. Then he joined him on the porch and they got down to business.

"Where is the bag? What's the plan now? What the fuck are we gonna do? Everything got turned upside down. We gotta talk this out. Do you have any suggestions?"

"Bags in the trunk. The plan is easy. Shoot 'em down. Burn the place. Go have a drink. See some titties at the bar."

"That is what you were supposed to do already. You fucked up."

"Well, to be honest, they kinda surprised me. They had someone helping them. I didn't expect them to start shooting. I'm not too happy about how things went down, either. It was supposed to be shooting fish in a barrel, but it was more like being chased by a pissed-off bull."

"Did you think they were too stupid to see you were setting them up? Junkies trust no one. They bring paranoia to a whole new level. You should have expected them to shoot at you. What would you have done if you were in their place?"

"I will take care of it. Everything is ready. Call them up and tell them where they can find their girl. Then this can all be finished."

"That would be great, but there is more to it than that, man. Lewis has lost it. He threatened to replace me. To replace us all. I'm not giving him a chance to make good on his threat. I want to replace him as the boss and run things myself from now on. Are you with me? You can be my right hand. I need someone I can trust beside me."

Bobby puffed on his cigarette, all quiet like, and looked out across the field into the darkness that was almost starting to glow with morning light. He seemed to be lost deep in thought. He didn't look like a man thinking over multiple murders and arson. You would have expected a madman with crazy hair pointing in all directions and a cackling laugh, but this was the opposite. Quiet. Calm.

Thomas spoke a little louder; his voice carried. "Hey, Bob, Hello, anybody home? Are you listening to me? Did you hear what I said? What say you, we a team or what?"

Bob flicked away his cigarette butt over the edge of the porch railing into the raindrops falling off the edge of the gutter. "Yeah, man, I got your back. It's high time for some big changes around here. It has been for a while now. Can I pick my team? No more Jims, and I'm all in."

"Glad you see it my way. No more Jims would be fine with me. Jim was an ass. Lewis kept him around. Another reason I want to run things. I don't want any more Jims either. If he would have done his job watching your back, you might have been able to do your job properly. His own choices, his mistakes, cost him his life and nearly yours, too. That's the game. I don't make the rules."

"We need new blood. Things around here have gotten stale, boring. We can make a lot more money than we are now. We can expand our reach. New territory, new staff, more money."

"Now that's the kind of talk I like to hear. I've been trying to go in that direction, but Lew has just been too old-goat stubborn to listen to me. What good is having a business manager if you won't listen to him? It's time to grow."

Thomas gestured slowly, widely, as if he was calling a great kingdom into existence from the scrubby trees. "Once word gets out we are in power and a growing force that is hiring only the best and brightest thieves, drug dealers, hottest whores and pimps, we should have a lineup of new guys and girls wanting to work for us. Always more money to be made when you get in on the ground floor. Everyone will want a piece of such a powerful new enterprise. We just have to get through the next couple of hours, and it will all be ours."

"Sounds great to me."

The two men shook hands. They even hugged. It meant more because they were men, sober men didn't hug each other without meaning. Sober man hugs were real. They would be close partners, and a hug proving mutual trust was a good way to start.

"It's time for me to put the bag in my car and make a couple of phone calls. First one to Sam and the next to Lew. Our plan stays the same, with one addition, shoot them all, including Lew, and burn the entire place to the ground. Go double-check and make sure you have everything set up to burn fast and hot."

He favoured Bobby with one of his big-city smiles. "This time you might get to see the fire burn a little."

51: Bigger things to worry about

Trisha fuckin' hated armchair athletes and, in this case, yet another bar stool brainiac. All talk and no action, fucking assholes is what they were. Yap yap yap, never-ending. No matter the topic they "knew how to", "knew a guy that" or "was there once when". If she had to stand there, smile and listen to one more how-fucking-to she would lose her mind.

She usually could keep her cool, but she was so worried.

Trisha often wondered where people got their ideas. Most people believed such crazy things that she thought they must have dreamed them. You could never shake them in their beliefs. They believed themselves to be all-knowing like they were preaching the holy gospel. Intelligent people had intelligent conversations. Idiots spouted false knowledge and spread their ignorance far and wide.

You could never change their minds or enlighten them. You might as well talk to the wall. The best thing to do was tune them out and not even acknowledge their pitiful existence. If no one argues or fights with them they move on to a new target. She had learned you often looked smarter by keeping your mouth shut.

It was sad that many of these people somehow had the chance to reproduce. She hoped if they had offspring that the kids would be more brainy than their parents. If not, this species was doomed. In a few generations, the population would be a bunch of drooling morons. Each with a purple participation ribbons and a pink shirt, sitting in their own drool.

She had heard it all in her years at the club, and all throughout school. There was always one egotistic asshat who had to run his mouth like he was a Ph. D. in about everything. One more bullshit story about nothing would be the one that would break the camel's crooked back.

"Shut the fuck up, Rick!" she yelled at the guy still sitting at the bar. "It's closing time, get your drunk ass outta here."

She was a little more shrill than she intended but didn't seem to bother him at all. He laughed and slid off the high bar stool. He staggered when his feet hit the floor and almost fell on his face. He did a kind of wobbly step with a little twirl. She couldn't believe he stayed on his feet, now *that* was an alcoholic. Lots of years of practice walking drunk, while trying not to look so drunk.

One dancer came over, smiled, and lead him by the arm to the cab waiting at the front door. One always showed up at closing time: there was always someone needing a ride. Rick would be back again tomorrow night and the night after that. He always came back. He wasn't a big spender, but he was a regular. Drank draft all evening and watched the people go by. Everyone knew Rick.

This was the way the night usually ended. Normally she could handle it all with a smile and nod, and sometimes she even teased them back, but not tonight. All the paying customers were gone. All that it left her with was the bottom of the barrel. The absolute bottom. She could stand most people, even drunk people, but full-of-shit blowhards wore her happy mask thin real fast. Especially since all she could think about was Adam.

The garbage bag she had stuffed in the trunk of her car, under her spare tire, wasn't helping at all.

She had expected to see Denise or even Thomas when she got back from Denise's, but neither of them was anywhere to be seen. She had to fight with herself to finish working and not run out the door in a mad panic.

The bouncers shooed the last patron off into the darkness, and she could finally shut the bar down and leave. She would come in early tomorrow and restock everything. The alarm could take care of the place for a few hours. She had bigger things to worry about. Trisha could think better at home in her tiny bachelor's apartment; there was no point staying at the club.

Trish knew she wouldn't be sleeping tonight. She would make herself a nice cup of hot tea, try to calm down, and make some phone calls. She hoped the sunrise would bring Adam back to her. She tried not to think of him while she was driving, or she would start crying and crash the car.

She didn't take long to get home; she sped a little. It was usually only twenty minutes from work to her apartment. That was half the reason she lived there. This time she made it in thirteen. There was no traffic or cops at this time of night. So the one thing she wasn't worried about right now was her speed.

She drove all the way home without stopping and, as most nights, didn't even meet one car. The only ones out this late at night were fools or up to no good. She let out a sigh of relief when she turned in the short driveway. She had been holding her breath and hadn't even noticed.

It was a shitty apartment on the edge of nowhere, but it was hers. She didn't mind the small place, since most of the time she was there alone. Even when Adam was there with her, it didn't feel cramped; it felt cozy.

She couldn't get Adam on his cell, or Sam either. Fuckin' phones. What fuckin' good were they, anyway?

She was panicking. Adam had told her to stay calm, but she couldn't help it. She knew that Thomas had to be out looking for the heroin, If she could get to him in time, she might save Sam, Adam and Jane.

She couldn't wait any longer for Thomas. Lewis was the one running shit anyway. Thomas wasn't the boss, no matter how much he acted like he was. If she had any chance of saving anyone, she had to get through to Lewis. She had found his number in Thomas' office. When she typed the numbers into her phone, her hands shook so bad she had to start over twice. Stupid touch screen. She hoped she wasn't too late.

No answer. Could he be home sleeping? This was all Denise's fault. Trisha might not be in her 20s or even her 30s anymore, but If she ever saw Denise again, she would kick her ass.

52: Looking

Lewis's cell phone buzzed in his pocket. He dug for it with his left hand while he steered the truck with his right. He thought it was Thomas calling in to tell him some good news.

The screen showed a number he didn't recognize. He always ignored unknown callers. This time he answered; there probably were no telemarketers calling at 4 am. "Yeah. Who is this?"

"Hi, is this Lewis?"

"Yeah. This better be good."

"This is Trisha. I work at the club."

"Your point is?"

"I'm sorry. I'm kind of nervous. I found something you are looking for. Something my boyfriend Adam lost."

"You have, have you? That *is* interesting. Where are you right now?"

"I'll give it to you if you promise not to hurt Adam. He is a great guy." Her voice broke. "I'll do whatever you want. Please don't hurt him. I know he's a fuck-up, but he's my fuck-up. Can we work something out?"

"Sure, whatever you say. Tell me where you are and I'll come to see you and we can talk."

"Okay, thank you. I live in the apartment building on the old Wharf Road. Used to be an old school. I live in apartment 3a. You know the place?"

"I'll be there as soon as I can get there. Lock your

doors and don't let anyone in. See you soon."

Surprise, surprise, Thomas had fucked up again. Or else this bitch was lying to him. Did she really have the drugs? Or was this a setup? He had no choice; he had to go check it out.

He knew Trisha; she had worked at his club for years. They weren't friends, but they were aware of each other. She didn't dance, so he didn't pay her much attention. He liked his girlfriends much younger and bustier. It had been a long time since she had seen her thirties.

Thomas had hired her, and she had been behind the bar ever since. He didn't know what to expect from her. One thing he knew, she was desperate, and you could never trust desperate people.

His plan remained the same. Get the heroin, from whoever the fuck had it, kill the witnesses, destroy the evidence. No witnesses or bodies meant no case.

Lewis turned the truck around and headed for the old school. He couldn't wait for this night to end.

He lit another cigar and coughed so hard of the first puff he almost passed out. The cigars were killing him, and the years of cigarettes before that. It was too late now.

No reason to quit now, though, just because he was coughing up blood. He would smoke till he couldn't hold a damned cigar anymore.

53: Good intentions

Lewis parked his truck close to the apartments, but far enough that it couldn't be seen from the windows. In case some nosey-Ned neighbour got up for a drink of water and looked outside and saw a truck in the yard.

It wasn't a big building, two stories, four apartments, so it only took a minute to find Trisha's apartment. 3a. Great, it was upstairs.

Stairs were not his friend. He was old and tired, but his knees were older. Had to be on the second floor. Fuck, this, like everything else, was going to take longer than he expected. Lewis hoped he could make it up there without taking a coughing fit and passing out.

He didn't have to be buzzed in, there wasn't even a lock on the front door to the place. Lew used a light touch when he knocked on the door. He didn't want to wake the whole place.

This would not take long. It took him longer to climb the staircase. He would be in and out and back on the road in no time flat. It didn't bother him that he knew Trisha for years. It wasn't his fault she got mixed up in this.

He heard a quiet "come in" from inside the apartment. He stood to one side and opened the door.

It was pitch dark inside. This was looking like a trap, so he didn't go any further into the room. He stayed in the hall by the doorway. "Trisha, you here? It's me, Lewis."

"Yes, Lewis. I'm here, and I have your fuckin' drugs."

He heard the quiet rustle of someone moving and the loud click of the hammer being pulled back on a gun. Sounded like a big gun. He backed away from the doorway another step farther.

"Adam told me the whole story. I know everything. He thought you would try to have him killed. Where is my boyfriend Adam? He's not answering his phone."

"He's gone to the cabin to get that other girl. You know the phones never work right here in a storm." He had to keep her believing until he got his hands on the bag.

"I want to see him, I need to know he's okay. Then you can have your bag of shit. I hid it. It's not here. It's far away. No one else knows where. So you can't kill me and take it. I'm not fuckin' stupid. I've been kicking around this pile of rocks long enough to know better."

"Why should I believe you, anyway? My trust isn't blind, sister. You could be a distraction. This little meeting could be a setup. The guys said they had the bag. Why would they lie? They know I'd catch on and make them pay a damn big price for lying and stealing from me."

"Yeah, well, they didn't have it. In case you haven't noticed, those two aren't the brightest bulbs, even when they are straight. You know that's why Thomas picked them in the first place: they were dumb jail cover dummies. I told Adam not to work for Thomas. I fucking told him. I knew it would lead to shit. Only it was worse than I thought. They didn't get busted; they got robbed. Someone stole the bag from them, and then I stole it from the bitch stealer. I'm not giving you a chance to steal it from me until I have proof that Adam is okay. When I see him and we leave together. I'll text you where to find your shit. I don't want it. Kill me here and you'll never find it."

"Easy, woman, calm your tits. Come with me and I'll

take you to him. There is no problem. You could even follow me to the cabin in your own car if you want, but I don't think it will get all the way through the rough road. It is far in the woods."

He doubted she hid the bag well or "far away". It was inside the apartment or in her car. If she even had it. He couldn't be sure if she was lying; she seemed pretty fucking serious.

She definitely knew too much about his business. She would have to come with him. Let her think it was her own idea. He would take care of her at the cabin with the others. He could send someone back here later and find the bag, if he found out she was telling the truth and the guys didn't have it.

"My gutless, little shit box of a car won't make it through a mud puddle. It has bald tires, and it runs best going downhill. Stopping at the bottom is iffy, I'll go with you. Remember you don't get the bag till Adam and I are safe and far from you and any of your friends."

"This isn't the way it was supposed to be. This isn't how I do business. I like to make my money quietly. Adam and Sam fucked this deal up. It should have been done and over with in a few minutes and they never even showed up! It shows me they have no respect for me or my business associates. I can't have that. That has to be dealt with. They have to disappear, leave town and never come back. If I get back what they lost, I'll call it even and we can go back to the way everything was before. They give me my stuff and I'll spare their shitty lives." He had always been a good liar. Especially when he was telling women what they wanted to hear.

"No way, I don't trust you any farther than I can throw you. I've worked for you for a decade, and while I haven't seen your ugly mug around much, I've heard the whispers. I know the stories. There is no going back to the way it was. We're done. Once I see Adam, we are leaving town and you won't see us ever again. Fuck Sam, his chick, the club and the rest of you."

His cell phone rang. He thought he'd set it to silent; guess it had slipped his mind. It startled him, and he jumped a little. So much for being the big, scary bad guy. He was kind of glad no one could see him right then.

He cleared his throat. "Can I answer my phone?"

"Go ahead. Maybe it's about Adam and Sam."

He dug the cell phone out of his back pocket. Another unknown number. Why not? He was on a roll tonight. What new shitstorm was going on now?

He swiped the screen to answer. "Yeah, this is Lewis. This better be fucking good."

54: Too soon

Sara should have known better than to fall for a chick with baggage. Everyone had exes, but this was too much. Look at the horror show she was dealing with now. She hoped they could get out of this mess alive.

Sara didn't know why she took the bag. Being impulsive was not one of her better qualities. She had been drunk, too drunk, and anger at Sam had blinded her. She had only seen red. Sara wanted a little revenge for Denise but she hadn't thought it through at all.

It was time to give the shit back to Lewis and be done with it. She knew who ran this place. She wanted to save her own ass, as well as Denise and even Sam, since he was Mikey's father.

She had to talk to the boss; she knew him well enough. She had spent a few nights in his bed when she first arrived in town. That was how she had gotten the job at the club. It was how most girls got their start at the club.

It was a special interview. A bedroom test that all the ladies had to pass, and she had passed with flying colours. She believed the lies of being a movie star, and this job would open all the right doors for her. It paid well, but the only door it opened are ones that should have stayed closed.

Drunk Sara had thought it would be a good way for Sam to get his ass kicked if he was a little late dropping the bag off. Now sober, she realized that this was going to get someone killed. His wallet was all she had set out to steal, not his life. This wasn't a joke.

She wanted to get rid of it as fast as she could. She would not wait for Denise to deal with it in the morning. She would go crazy with anxiety if she waited. She had taken the bag, she would take the risk to give it back. She had a key to Denise's.

She dialed Lewis' number. It rang and rang. So she tried again. Nothing. God, she hated being ignored. She tried once more, and this time Lew answered.

"What?"

"It's Sara, I have your stuff stashed at my girlfriend's place. Come pick me up and we can go get it. I'll explain everything then. Hurry up. I live at 76 Water Street. Second door on the right."

She hung up and sat down to wait for him to arrive.

When she was a little girl, she had dreams of being a dancer, a real dancer. A ballerina in a beautiful costume bringing people to tears with the beauty of her footsteps. Dreams of being showered with roses, not a washed-up porn star, lucky these days to get a twenty-dollar tip.

Deep down, she knew girls like her didn't get to dance *Swan Lake*. Like her mother had always been sure to remind her, even when she was sick and dying: Sara was no good, like her no-good father.

All her family did her entire life was drink and fight. They cared about her enough to argue whose fault it was that she had left. But that was it, she was a weapon they all used to cut each other.

No wonder she had ended up here stripping. She wanted to be loved by everyone. She had a deep-need to please and be accepted by those around her. When she was growing up, it seemed she could never do good enough, never be good enough. She overcompensated by being a pushover and letting people talk her into doing things she didn't want to. By the time she figured out she was being used, it was too late.

Sara was barely twenty. Bad decisions were her specialty. Drinking and making bad decisions. Taking the bag of heroin was another one of those bad choices Drunk Sara was very good at making.

Denise didn't use her. Denise might have loved her a little. Meeting Denise, her dream girl, had turned into a nightmare. The wrong place at the wrong time was the story of her life. She told herself she didn't care what "they," thought. But she always went out of her way to please someone. New friends, old friends, anyone at all.

They all wanted the same thing from her. Sex. She had a beautiful body. Sex was a way to show love. She always gave in. The other person, man or woman—she'd been burnt by both sexes—always moved on to the next dumb girl, leaving Sara to wonder why and agonize over what she could have done to make them stay. She never felt good enough for anyone.

Only when she met Denise did she feel like she had met someone real. Someone who wanted nothing from her. Sure they had sex. But they also talked, laughed and ate together. They had been keeping their new relationship a secret. So what? It was their business. They weren't hiding it because they were ashamed; They were enjoying each other and didn't want to share their joy with anybody else.

Sara was a few years younger than Denise. They had both been served their share of shit sandwiches, and neither of them wanted any more.

What if their boss asked them to make out on stage? Chicks at the club did it all time, even ones who weren't gay or couples. They looked at it like acting and a way to make more money. But a couple on stage wasn't going to happen. At least not this couple. Money wasn't enough.

It was a lie. Money was what she had seen when she took the heroin. A big pile of money they could use to make a new start, a new life in a new town or city, it didn't matter where they lived. If she could be with Den forever, she'd live on a mountaintop. Seeing no one else again.

That had been her dream, for a little while at least.

55: Dirt roads

How he, Lewis, the fucking boss, was taxiing around bartenders at gunpoint at 4 am was out of his range of comprehension. He was more than pissed off. He was furious, but kept his composure.

He knew how to handle himself. He didn't want to upset Trisha any more; she was already wound up.

How was he going to take care of Sara while Trisha was with him? She knew where Sarah lived; Everyone knew everything around here. She'd know something was up if he took her there, especially right now. She had to be smart enough to know it was all connected.

But maybe not, maybe he would get lucky. Or maybe she would be so worried about her so-called "man" she wouldn't notice or care what he was up to.

The only way was to blindfold her, so she didn't know where they were going. Or shoot her now. If she didn't see what he was up to, she couldn't freak out.

He knew he'd have to talk her into it. If he just tried to blindfold her, she was liable to shoot him right there. She had a quick temper and took no shit. That was one reason she'd worked for him for so long.

This was the last thing he needed to be doing. He paid people to do this. His people were slipping, getting sloppy. Their focus wasn't at work, their minds were drifting somewhere else. Maybe in a bed with a woman, exactly where his sick ass should be.

It all had to be done, though. If he did it, at least he would know it was done right. He'd be at the cabin soon enough, and he'd be able to shut her up for good.

Too bad, she had always been a good employee; she helped keep the girls from ripping each other's heads off. There were lots of cat fights and jealousy on most nights.

He could find a new mama/manager next week. For now, he had to focus on convincing her that she and her loser boyfriend would see the sunrise. Or he could just shoot her now and have someone tear apart her apartment.

Decisions, decisions. Guess that was why he was the boss.

"Look, Trisha, I have to make a quick stop."

"What do you mean 'a quick stop'? What in the hell is more important than this?"

"I can't tell you, and I can't show where we're going, either. You will have to trust me. One of those 'If I told you I'd have to kill you' kinda things. You'll have to wear a blindfold."

"Fuck you, blindfold. To make it easier for you to take me out in the woods and shoot me?"

"Honey, you should know. I don't need to put a blindfold on you to shoot you." He pulled back his jacket, so she could see the metallic shine of a handgun snuggled in a black leather holster. "I could do it right now and not you or anybody else in the world could stop me."

"Same goes for you, buddy. My gun might be in my pocket, but it is pointed right at you. At this range, I can't miss, even if I tried. Whichever one of us pulls the trigger first wins the race, Mr. Cowboy. I'm ready."

"Smart lady, that's why I like you. We are going to have to trust each other."

"Great. Trust. That has always worked out great for me

so far."

She lit a cigarette, blew the smoke out the passenger side window. "Do what you gotta do along the way. Hurry your old ass up and take me to my man."

"Sit there like a lady and keep your big trap shut and you'll do fine."

Lewis left town and headed for the cabin. He was still deciding what to do with Trisha. It hardly mattered where the heroin was anymore. Regardless, people had to be held responsible, even if they weren't.

He was sending a big message out tonight that would not be misunderstood. If you fuck with Lewis, you get you were going to lose everything. The list of bodies of former employees was getting longer. At least the guys weren't on any official payroll.

Trisha was different. She could be connected to him. These bodies would have to disappear. He didn't like the sound of that, though. Without dead bodies to scare people, he wasn't sending a message at all. Maybe some would disappear and some be found.

"I can't believe you kidnapped Jane. She doesn't deserve any of this shit. She never took your stuff."

"Not my problem, doll. Who she spends her time with is her problem. Guilty by association."

"If she took your bag, then I'd agree, but she didn't do shit and you know it. You're the ass who can't control his staff. Just a god-damned bully."

That was the last straw. Not dealing with this shit anymore. He jammed on the brakes hard, and had his gun out as she bounced against her seat belt. He shot her twice in the body and once in the head.

Finally, it was fucking quiet in the truck for the first time since he picked her up. The tension was gone. He could finally think. He'd bring her along and dump her with the rest.

Lewis pulled over to the side of the road and tossed her limp body into the bed of the truck like it was a bag of garbage. To him that all it was.

One more problem solved. Of course, it created the problem of hiring a new bartender, but no worry. He would have Thomas take care of that.

He called one of the low-level goons to go to Trisha's place and see if they could turn up any bags of goodies. He went to see what Sara had to say.

56: Next

Sara met Lewis at the door. He was old but still strong and heavy. He grabbed her and pushed her back through the doorway into the house. They tripped over a cat and went sprawling. Lewis landed on top, and something broke with a sharp snap, possibly one of her ribs.

"I got a lot of shit to do so I'm only gonna say this once. Where is my bag bitch?"

"Not here," she gasped. "At Denise's place. I hid it in her bathroom closet. I took the bag. I was just trying to fuck with Sam. I didn't want to get him in this much trouble."

"Okay. I'll have someone go pick it up and you won't have to worry about it anymore."

He stood up slowly, watching her press her hands over her ribs. She opened her mouth to say something, and he shot her in the chest and head. Not in her pretty face, but in the head. He always shot twice to be sure.

She was a fucking thief. He wasn't keeping her around to steal from him again. She would not be a wife or mother or own her own car or house. In the grand scheme of the universe, she wouldn't be missed. Her list of accomplishments wasn't long at all. She had finished high school. Would anyone remember that? All she would be remembered for was being shot in the head. And for stripping, that would never be forgotten. Empowered women with confidence and strength to make money from their bodies were never remembered for anything else.

Society was a bitch that way.

It all ended with Lew's bullets. If she hadn't called him, she would have lived at least until morning, or even the next day. Sooner or later they would have figured out it was her who took the bag of heroin in the first place.

Her death was a sure thing from the second she touched that bag. Her body would be cold by the time the sun came up.

57: Bag boy

It surprised Chris when his phone buzzed after work. He was getting ready to go to bed. It was late. It always took him a little while to wind down after a night shift at the station.

This shift had been a doozy. The first 911 call came in around 3 am. Teenagers went to an abandoned fish plant to smoke a joint, have a drink, and try to find their way into each other's pants. All they found was a dead guy.

It was out of the ordinary for a body to turn up in the area. Everyone was in high gear. Once the police got some light on the place they found a second dead guy. This one looked like a skinny junkie, but there wasn't enough left to ID him. They were gonna need fingerprints to identify this guy. He had more than one bullet hole in him.

Things had gone bad at this place, very bad. It was going to take a while to figure out what connection the two dead men had.

The second emergency call came in at 4 am, about a third body at a second location. This time a woman, found by a hysterical neighbour. They had to scramble to call in everyone. Almost all of them tired and on overtime. They were gonna need a lot of coffee. The whole year's budget would get spent fast if dead bodies kept turning up.

Everybody was at the party. People would talk about this bash for a while. Rookies, the night shift, the day shift, even the Captain had to get out of his warm bed.

The coroner's office, police photographers, even firemen came along to make sure it was safe when the cops found evidence of attempted arson at the first scene.

It wasn't long before the news vans and photographers showed up, with reporters trying to get a shot of a body bag or any minuscule detail they could spin into a story.

Dead bodies and overtime made the top brass angry. The force was always spread pretty thin; that was normal. Budget blah blah, never enough government money. They always seemed to be shorthanded, even on a good day when the body count stayed at zero. It was the same at every department. Not enough money, not enough cops.

With the phones ringing off the hook, no one noticed at first that John wasn't right in the middle of things. John was usually around. All he did was work. He lived alone and spent most nights, even off-duty ones, in his windowless office, drinking coffee and doing paperwork. John wasn't answering his phone.

The only reason anyone thought of him was because they knew he was working a new missing-persons case and first they thought maybe the dead girl was the girl he was looking for. They couldn't even contact the lady who had filed the missing person report. No answer on any of the contact info she provided. It was as if she disappeared, like her sister. They looked in John's office and couldn't even find the files.

It was the rookie who had the brainwave to try to track his cell number. They were the police. They rarely tracked each other, but they could, with ease. As long as the person they were tracking left the phone on, or at least had the battery in it. Then they'd know where his phone was, or had been last, even if they didn't know exactly where he was. They could tell the last tower it pinged from even if it had died or been shut off since then. Pings don't lie.

They sent a squad car out to where they last got a ping from John's phone. You never know: the old fella might have had a heart attack, or maybe he had picked up a new lady friend and was having a piece of strange. Either way they had to find him.

Once Chris couldn't stay awake anymore the Captain told him to go home. He followed orders. He had taken a shower and had a sandwich and a relaxing cup of tea.

And then, out of the blue, the phone.

"Hello?"

"Hi, This is Lewis. Do you know who I am?"

"Yes, yes, I know who you are." Chris had never gotten a phone call from the boss before. He hadn't even met the boss.

"I need you to do a favour for me."

His dispatch job was pretty easy. He didn't have to get shot at; he got to stay at the station. He wanted to keep it, and the extra money Thomas had been giving him for the last few months to keep him posted on any info they might find interesting. He took the money, and passed on info that might help keep Thomas and Lewis on top of the game. Cops made shit pay. He couldn't refuse the boss: that was the racket he was in.

"Sure, boss. I can help you out."

"Do you know where Trish the bartender lives? Go to Trisha's house and turn it upside down and let me know if you find a bag. Like a gym bag, or something that size."

"Okay, sounds easy enough."

"Do you know what's in the bag?"

"Nope, I don't know what's in the bag, don't care either, long as I get a nice tip later."

"Good answer. Call me when you have something to

say that I want to hear."

"Will Trisha be home?"

"No, she won't be home. Don't worry about her. She won't come home and surprise you while you are there."

The line went dead. Chris put down his phone, finished his tea, got dressed and headed out across town for Trisha's apartment.

58: Outside

Lynda couldn't keep her mind from wandering while she walked in the dark woods. Words can be so hurtful, even when they aren't meant to be. Keeping things inside seemed easier than admitting the truth, even to yourself. Sometimes just talking is the hardest thing to do. You can't just wish bad things away.

Jane had tried, and it didn't get her anywhere. Sticking your head in the sand is never a good solution to any situation. Just because you don't want to believe something is true doesn't make it any less real. Bad things happen, and you have to deal with them. You move on.

Get help if you need it. If you don't, the things you hold inside and obsess over will slowly poison you and all your future relationships. The past is the past, it can't be changed. We make mistakes. We can't control everything. Sometimes things just happen, and nothing we try to do can stop it.

The only thing to do is learn from it. Let the pain go and move forward. If not, you might as well give up and jump off a bridge. The ending would be just as messy but would happen much faster and be easier on the family. Watching someone you love fall to pieces and slowly shatter, choosing to end their life, was devastating. It was a trauma worse than any physical wound.

That was the way it was with Jeremy. He came back home to her alive. It hurt him; he wasn't whole, but he was alive.

After his body healed. He walked around. He smiled. It was all an illusion. He had nightmares almost every night. Sometimes he even woke up screaming. Even though he was safe, his mind was sure he was still in danger. He was afraid he would hurt Lynda in one of these nightmare rages. Or the daytime rages. He was in constant pain; he took heavy painkillers just to be able to stand. They made him sick as a dog. He hated the way they made him feel.

He tried to get a medical marijuana license, but hadn't found a doctor willing to sign the papers. It was still taboo. Much like PTSD and mental illness in general. Unspoken, swept under the rug. His doctor felt all cannabis use was recreational.

He couldn't afford or find good strains of marijuana. Sometimes he would find one that improved his pain, but then in a few weeks it would be gone. Suppliers sold it all as fast as they could. It would leave Jeremy with nothing for his pain and he would have to rely on the pills again.

The government paid for them, no question: OxyContin, Dilaudid, whatever he needed for pain; Ativan for any anxiety. They paid for everything except for pot. That was still illegal.

Every few years a party trying to get into office would say it was going to legalize grass. It would almost happen and then the government would change, and it would start all over again.

If he could have had a pot license and the government would have taken care of its vets' physical and mental health properly, he might still be here with her. They would have had kids by now.

She tried not to think about what might have been, the joys and the sorrows. The past was over. She had to let it go or she would end up as sick as Jeremy had been. Mental illness was so common and the stigma surrounding it and getting treatment wasn't getting any better. So many hurting people needed help and didn't know how to get it. So many ended up living on the streets. Even loving, caring families had a hard time helping their loved ones' suffering. Lots of times the sick person ends up alone & homeless, needing more help than before and just hitting brick walls. So many, just like her Jeremy, died for nothing.

In the months following his return from active duty, he wasn't living, just going through the motions. He was trapped in the memories of the terrible things he had seen. He never really came back.

Two other guys that were on the same mission with him died, and Jeremy blamed himself for living. Why? Why them and not him?

He would fly into a rage at nothing at all. He'd smash and break things. He would be genuinely sorry afterwards but it was scary when it happened.

He felt like he was losing his mind. He thought there must have been something he could have done differently to save them. No matter that he had been wounded himself, that he lost part of himself.

It wasn't logical; it was an illness. Jeremy knew he was sick and tried to get help, but the help he needed just wasn't available. He talked to doctors, told them everything he was feeling and how he was acting. Their answer was pills. So he took the pills.

He tried. Lynda loved him. It wasn't enough. He couldn't cope with living that way anymore, fearing he would hurt Lynda or someone else, so he hung himself in the garage one day while Lynda was at work.

The note he left just said, "I'm sorry. It's better this way. Love Jeremy."

Was Jane stronger than Jeremy? Could she come back from this? Could she recover from the kidnapping? Could Jane make it through this day and the next and the ones after that? She would be scarred. Hell all of them will be.

Lynda steeled her resolve, if she could survive the death of their parents and bringing Janie up on her own, if she could survive finding her husband hanging lifeless in the garage, then she could get Jane and herself through this.

All those events hurt her almost to madness. She made it through because of her little sister. She had to take care of her. There was no one else.

They just had to survive, and then they could deal with what came after, later. If any of them could survive this fucking mess.

Could Lynda? She had killed a man. Killed him. Well, she thought she did. He stopped coming after her when she pushed him backwards.

She had lucked out. When she pushed all her weight against him, it wasn't much. She only weighed about 115 pounds soaking wet. But he tripped on an old board.

That was the universe, karma, or just plain luck, whatever you wanted to call it, knocking him off balance. Pure bad luck for him that the rebar had been there.

She didn't mean to kill him; she didn't think. Well, maybe she meant to. Deep down she knew it was her or him, and she would bet on her.

She tried to tell herself she had had no choice; she knew she had had no choice, but it still fucked with her head.

It had been dark inside the old plant, but she had seen the metal sticking into the back of his head, and blood dripping down, soaking his blue shirt collar.

She pushed those thoughts away and tried to focus on

just getting through the next few hours of her life. They could worry about what happens later, later.

59: Reunion

John and Sam ran down the road toward the cabin, staring hard into the darkness around them until they saw spots as they tried to see enemies or wild animals that might be waiting for them. The darkness seemed to be crawling with darker shadows, it was alive.

Sam went first, with John close behind. The slimy mud was slick even if you were walking, and they had a hard time keeping on their feet. The rain had finally stopped but the wind was still blowing hard. At least it was drying their wet clothes a little. The pine needles under their feet were as slippery as ice and the muck underneath the carpet of years and years of fallen orange needles pulled at their shoes, threatening to leave them travelling in their sock feet. More than once they had to stop to fish one of their shoes out of the mud.

Sam didn't care if he had to crawl. He was getting to that cabin and Jane. He would gladly crawl through hell for her. He realized if he didn't love her more than himself, he just would have hit the road and never looked back. He was a better person than that. Maybe not a smarter person, but better.

"We're getting close to the building," John said quietly. "I can see a porch light up ahead. Real considerate of Bobby to leave a light on for us,"

"We might as well go in together. They know you were with me at the warehouse."

"You go first. You do the talking, since this is your mess. Jane is your girl, and you know these guys better than I do. I'll try to hang back and cover you."

"What, you don't have brunch with them every Tuesday?"

John laughed. "Not quite, brunch usually isn't my thing. Or lunch. Coffee. Coffee, coffee, that's me."

"I'm so damn cold and wet, coffee would be great even though I never got a taste for it. More guns would be great, too, and a bunch of your police buddies."

"Sorry, no cop buddies in sight. Looks like it's just the two of us. Let's go get Jane and later I'll treat you to the strongest, hottest, cuppa joe in town."

"Sounds good to me, my friend," Sam said. "We'd better go. I think the time is now."

They didn't bother hiding anymore. They just walked right up the driveway and knocked on the front door. They were expected. They felt busting the door in would be a little too Dirty Harry. They went in a little quieter than that.

The door swung inward a little on its own. It moved so slow that Sam wanted to kick it in, but he waited.

The door opened further, revealing Jane still tied to a chair. She had blood on her face and clothes; drops of it had even dried on the gag in her mouth, and some had run from a cut over her eye and stained her blindfold. She was shaking back and forth. That was all she could do.

Sam tried to run to her, but John grabbed him and held him back for just a fraction of a second, and a bullet whizzed by right in front of his nose.

John lost his grip on the wet jacket and Sam dove across the room to land beside Jane's chair. John stayed crouched by the door, trying to see where Bobby was hiding. He fired a few random shots around the room to cover Sam, who was trying his best boy scout act to rescue Jane.

If Sam had been a boy scout, he would have brought a knife to cut the ropes. They were so close, but they still had less than a snowball's chance in hell of making it out of there without extra holes in their bodies.

Sam couldn't breathe for a few seconds. He almost froze in horror from what Jane had been through because of him. The pictures and video had not prepared him for this.

When he could get himself moving, he pulled the gag and blindfold off Jane's bruised and battered face, trying to go fast but gentle. He covered her with kisses, crying like a baby the whole time. "I'm so sorry baby, I love you. I'm so sorry, baby, I love you."

She was crying, too. Tears of joy and relief. Her voice was a raspy croak from screaming and having nothing to drink since forever. "I can't believe you're here, are you for real?"

He tried to untie the ropes. He winced at how deep they were digging into the soft skin of her wrists, arms, and legs. He wished he had a knife.

Then Bobby crashed into him, seeming to come out of nowhere. One second he was kissing Jane, the next he was he was flying across the floor with Bobby stuck to him like glue. Bob wasn't very big, but he hit like a truck.

Sam throat-punched him. It only slowed Bobby down a little. Sam tried to roll away, but he had to stop rolling when he hit the wall.

The collision between Bob and Sam had knocked Jane down. She landed on her side, still half-tied to the chair, just missing the thick, steel edge of the welded steel wood rack beside the cold stone fireplace. She started screaming words of encouragement like "kill him", "shoot him", "watch out".

Sam didn't think her coaching was helping his strategy. At least as long as she was screaming, he knew she was alive.

Sam and Bobby rolled around the floor, crashing into furniture, knocking over a small table and shattering lamps and ornaments. An extra-cute figurine of a little boy in shorts, suspenders and a little hat, with a fishing pole, flew in an arc past Jane, landing upright on the floor almost at the end of her nose, from her angle it must have looked like the boy was fishing for her. The way she was squirming and straining against her ropes she almost looked like a fish just out of the water trying to figure out why they couldn't breathe or swim in this new world.

Sam didn't see John get up from his spot on the porch and come into the cabin to try to help. But he heard the gunshots. As soon as John got close to the two wrestling men on the floor, he took a shot in the shoulder and one in the body and fell face-first to the floor beside them in a bloody heap.

Sam saw him hit the floor. He thought, *That's it, we're done, we are all going to die here tonight.*

A gun thundered again, and Bobby stiffened and stopped squeezing San's throat. He reached for his back.

Sam pushed him off, grabbed a chair and broke it over the back of the huge man who was holding Jane by her hair, making her scream a different scream. The chair broke into bits.

Thomas dropped Jane and turned to face Sam. It was like looking up at a giant. Sam wasn't a big guy to begin with, and all his partying of late hadn't helped him put any weight on. He was a rack of bones.

"I'll finish you myself," Thomas said. "I should have just shot you soon as you missed the drop, and not even bothered with this bitch."

Thomas turned back towards Jane. The look on his face was not a good one. It wasn't angry. It was past anger. It was cold, like a huge iceberg crushing the hull of a boat. No emotion, just cold.

Out of the corner of his eye Sam saw Lynda with a gun. She looked like she might pass out. Her skin was white against the dried blood from the wound on her head. He backed in her direction. Anything to get away from the snarling beast looming over him.

"Shoot him, Lynda! NOW!"

"I'm scared to hit you or Jane!"

"Just pull the trigger! You did it just right a minute ago. Just do it, breathe and pull!"

He continued to back towards her at a snail's pace. Just as his elbow was nearing the end of her outstretched arms, a shot rang out and she pitched forward with blood pouring out of her arm. She dropped the gun and it went spinning across the room, far away from Sam again.

Thomas smiled and picked the still-tied-up Jane up by her hair. She screamed.

60: A walk in the woods

John had tried his best to drive to where the GPS said the cabin was, but there was no way Jane's little car would make it past the deep ruts. No matter how many times the computer voice said turn right here, he couldn't go down that road. It had been dry all summer and this one storm seemed to dump the whole seasons' worth of water all at once.

They left the car on the side of the road. With luck, they could make it back here before too long. She would see her sister soon; she could feel it.

John and Sam were ahead of her. They thought she might be safer that way. They had told her to stay in the car and to be ready to leave in a hurry when they got back. They expected the car to be running. The keys were in it, so whoever got there first could drive. But she would not wait in the car, she wasn't a dog.

Lynda was walking through the thick woods in the strange, pre-light of almost-dawn when she heard the first gunshot, and before the sound had died away another shot rang through the woods. Great. Things seemed to go exactly the way she expected. It didn't take long to kick off; The guys were only about five minutes ahead of her and already guns were going off. She hoped her sister was okay. She had to be.

She moved faster, trying to find the cabin. The guys had run up the side of the dirt drive; she took to the woods. Trying to stay undercover. Great idea. If anyone was looking for intruders, they would hear her from a mile away. Swearing and crashing around the woods like a bull moose.

It was hard going trying to push past the dense underbrush, pricker bushes and damned burdocks. They were the worst, and she had no one to pull them off her back. How did they always end up tangled in her hair? If Jane was here, they would have helped each other.

She wasn't dressed for hiking, either, in an old pair of jeans, a sweater, sneakers, and a light jacket. Not much defence against the sharp branches and thorns. Each time a branch pulled her hair a bolt of pain shot through her head.

She knew she should have gone to the hospital, but it was too late now. She had to keep going; She had to get to Jane.

As Lynda broke through the stand of stunted spruce at the edge of the treeline, the smell of smoke wafted towards her. It reminded her of campfires and s'mores. Happy thoughts didn't fit in with what was happening to her right now.

She stopped at the edge of the woods and watched the cabin for a few minutes, waiting for any more shooting. Now she could see clouds of smoke and the glow of flames coming from behind the building.

There were two cars in the yard, one of them full of bullet holes and broken windows. The other was a newer, nicer, shinier model. Not a scratch on it, parked out front. She didn't see anyone around at all.

Still, she waited a few more minutes. At the warehouse, she had been way too careless and had almost gotten herself killed. She was trying to be stealthy and sneaky.

Between her and the cabin there was nothing for her to hide behind. She had to hope no one looked outside when she was crossing the old pasture. She ducked down and ran through the field like her feet were on fire.

She made it across without being shot. She let out the breath she hadn't even been aware she'd been holding.

Once she reached the cars, she hunkered down behind them to catch her breath. Then she did a second sprint to the porch, getting up on it as quietly as possible so she could peek at a window.

This was starting to be a thing with her. First the warehouse, now the cabin, once more and it would be a pattern. Being a peeping Lyn didn't suit her very well. She was always a very private person and tried to respect others' privacy. Never had she peeked into a window in her entire life before this all began. She didn't plan to do it ever again if she made it out of here alive.

Complete chaos spread across the canvass that had been a cute cabin when she peeked inside. It made her wonder if anyone from either side would leave this house at all. She hoped this place wasn't a mausoleum in disguise.

There was no need to worry about someone seeing her, they were all too busy trying to kill or save one another. An alien spacecraft could have landed, with flashing lights and howling sirens. No one would have noticed.

She had plenty of time to take in the entire scene. Lynda couldn't tell who was winning; everyone in the room looked like they were losing.

If not for Jane she would be far from anyone or anything like this. She avoided violent stories on news like the plague; it gave her nightmares to think of all the bad, random events in the world. It was better not to think about it at all.

Lynda looked around the porch for something she could use as a weapon. There was an old rocking chair, a small table. A big rock beside the front door that must have at one time have been a doorstop. It wasn't intimidating compared to a gun but it might have to do. She always had been an old school kinda gal.

Still, she would feel better if she had a real weapon. She went back to the two cars in the driveway, hoping to find something better there. She was desperate, anything that looked hard or sharp would do.

In the car with the bullet holes, she found nothing of use. Some crumpled take-out wrappers and trash. The car smelled of stale cups of coffee, and cigarettes. If whoever owned the car survived the night, but kept up their bad habits, they would soon meet their maker.

In the second car, she had better luck, finding an actual gun and bullets in the dash. Guns had always scared her. Now she wished she knew more. Seemed like it was an important thing to know, or the gun might as well be a rock with no bullets in it.

There were extra clips, heavy with bullets. She stuffed them in her pocket. The owner of this car had come prepared. He would be the one she had to watch for.

She would get her sister. She would shoot someone if she had to. More than one, all of them, whoever got in her way. How easy it was to decide to become a serial killer. Lynda couldn't wait any longer.

The back door seemed like a good plan. She ran to the back of the cabin, but it wasn't as good an idea as she thought.

As she reached the back yard there was an explosion. It wasn't super loud, but she felt a thump. The back door was hanging open. It looked like it had been torn from the hinges by some huge beast. At least she didn't have to open it, small miracles. Had to be grateful for them.

But to her dismay, as she got closer, she saw that most of the back of the building and half the woodpile were now burning. Soon the whole building would go up in flames. There was no going in that way, so back around to the front door it was.

She had to get Jane out of there before she got burned alive. The outlook for the morning kept getting better and better. Screw it.

She ran in through the front door with her gun raised.

61: Cooking

Lynda scrambled around on the kitchen floor. She scurried under the table like that was going to hide her skinny ass from anyone. Then she crawled over to the sink. This was a kitchen: there had to be a knife somewhere.

She stuck her shaking hands into the first drawer. Soft dishcloths. She wouldn't be able to kill anyone with these, but grabbed a couple to jam into the bullet hole in her arm. The second drawer was a jumble of mismatched Tupperware. Useless even in ordinary circumstances. No help there.

She was running out of drawers and time. She glanced up at the counter top and, lo and behold, there was a whole knife block full of kitchen weaponry.

The big butcher knife looked like a good bet, but she was afraid it was too big for her small hand. So instead she grabbed a sort of oversized steak knife. It had mean looking teeth and felt good in her hand. It looked and felt like it would hurt. She wrapped it in one of the dishcloths and shoved it in her jacket sleeve.

She was trying to grab a second knife for backup when a big hand grabbed her by the hair and dragged her out of the kitchen.

Guess he didn't want a sandwich. He pulled so hard she thought her scalp was going to come off her skull. She clawed at the huge hand gripping her hair. It was like trying to cut down a maple tree with her bare hands. She wished she could kick him, but she wasn't tall enough or flexible enough for that. Mental note: Join Wednesday night yoga classes again if she survived.

She didn't want to let him know she had the knife, she wanted to try to free Jane. Then if he found the knife, so be it, she'd bury it in his heart if she had to.

"Fucking let go!" Lynda screamed and flailed around at the end of his arm like a wild animal.

"Shut up!" he growled.

He threw her into the corner. She landed hard on her injured arm beside her sister. The pain almost made her pass out, but she was too happy to be close to Jane to let that happen. She hugged her as tight as she could. She kept her arm with the steak knife behind Jane.

"Go ahead cuddle all you want," coughed an old guy Lynda had never seen before. "Soon this shit will be all over, you won't have to worry about your sister anymore, you both will be smoke on the wind."

"Fuck you, old man."

"Under better circumstances, the three of us would have had a great time. Even though you aren't quite my type, I'd have made an exception to get little sister in the mix." Lewis started to laugh but ended up coughing again and spit bloody phlegm on the floor.

He wiped the bright red blood staining his mouth with a blue silk handkerchief. He glared at the two women huddled on the floor. He was trying to be scary. Like she could be any more scared. He looked like a b-movie vampire. His words scared her more than his look.

"Then I would have put your sister on the stage and then sent her into the VIP lounge. She'd work hard all night, every night. Maybe I still will. It's pretty easy to make a woman do what you want. A little chemical help and they'll sell their own kid."

He didn't seem to be watching them closely. Just sort of talking to the air. She slid the knife out of her sleeve and started to cut the ropes still binding Jane's hand to the chair. At least it had broken a few times. It was now missing a few legs so there was less of her still attached to it.

She whispered to Jane, "Stay still while I try to cut you free."

"Okay, Sis."

"Hurry," Sam hissed. "Maybe if we rush the old guy at once, we can get by him. We don't have a choice. We can't sit here and wait for him to shoot us."

"Do you think you can run, Janie?"

"I'll try. I'll do anything to get out of here."

Lynda sawed at the ropes while keeping her eyes on Lewis. He was so old it looked like a strong wind would blow him over. "When I say we all run."

62: No way out

This fucking chair might as well be a coffin. Jane was starting to believe she might never get out of it. There had been a slight glimmer of hope when Sam arrived, but that shining spark had dimmed. Like a star so far away, the harder you try to see it, the more blurry it becomes. That was how she saw her chances of surviving tonight. She could almost see it but it was hard.

She kept struggling to get free while the big man and Sam were fighting. She writhed around on the floor, still tied to the chair. It had splintered a bit the last time Thomas had dropped her.

Jane's shoulder was still throbbing from how hard she hit the floor. She hoped nothing important was broken. She tried not to think any more than that.

The cabin was an older place that was last redecorated some time in the 70s. Copious amounts of fluffy soft shag carpet everywhere. She landed hard enough to shatter one rung on the back of the chair, but not her spine.

Jane kept wiggling the broken rung even though part of it was sticking into the soft skin of her back. Finally, she worked one arm free of the rope. It hurt like hell to move her arm; it had been in the same spot for almost two days.

Jane kept moving her arm and fingers a little farther, a little farther. She scanned the room to see where everyone had ended up, and if anyone was looking her way. She tried to get her other hand free, but the knots were still holding tight on that side.

It was getting harder to see and breathe by the second. Whatever was on fire was getting worse and the entire room, the whole house, was filling up with smoke.

Lynda was nowhere to be seen. Maybe she was hiding in the kitchen, she had scurried off to some place safer than this room that already reeked of burnt gunpowder and death. Jane felt terrible that she had drawn her sister here. This was the last place she wanted Lynda to be.

The guy who shot Bobby wasn't moving. The big guy was fighting Sam again. Not really fighting; he was just choking the life out of Sam a little at a time. Sam was scratching and clawing at his bulging arms, trying to break free. It was like trying to tear down a tree with his bare hands; he wasn't having much luck. Sam's face was changing colours and his lips were turning blue.

With her free hand, all Jane could reach was that figurine of the little boy fishing. But she had played a lot of softball in her younger years. It had been fun to hang out with the boys and be more than a scorekeeper.

She threw the little man as hard as she could; she made a small grunt when she let the tiny guy loose.

It hit the giant right on the temple. It definitely wasn't a killing blow, but it distracted him enough that he took one hand off Sam's throat and flinched a little.

Sam took a huge gulp of air. He grabbed the poker from the fireplace and whacked at the big guy.

The first hit got the giant in the face. His left cheek busted open and blood poured down his chin and neck. A couple more of those solid hits, and he was almost free.

"Fuck you, Thomas!" Sam screamed in a high-pitched wheeze as he swung the poker in an arc again. His aim wasn't as good as Jane's and some blows glanced off the side of the man's big arm and shoulder.

Deafening gunshots rang out, causing Jane to scream again.

"That's quite enough!" an old man she didn't recognize was shouting. He punctuated his words with more gunshots.

Everyone in the room stopped moving. More out of stunned surprise than anything.

The old man nudged Sam with the tip of his shiny leather shoe. "You get the fuck over there with her, you lousy piece of shit."

Sam started crawling toward Jane. Slowly, like things were broken in him.

The old man turned his attention to Thomas, the giant. "Get whoever is hiding in the kitchen and put out whatever the fuck is on fire—for now. Where the fuck is Bobby, anyway?"

63: Final fight

Thomas waded through the heavy smoke, trying to find out what exactly was burning. He didn't know what contraption Bobby had rigged up. Maybe it was all smoke and no fire, but he doubted it. He didn't think he could stop whatever fiery end Bob had planned for the crack head and the girl.

He moved forward anyway; standing still would not help anyone. He couldn't see much or barely breathe.

Thomas wiped the blood out of his left eye. It was oozing from a deep cut on his forehead. It dripped down and mixed with the cut on his cheek and ran down his neck. One side of his face was a mask of blood. And for once it was his blood.

His head was pounding from the last few hits Sam had landed. That little fucker hit hard. He could at least respect that, if nothing else.

Tom didn't like to admit it, but he knew he was lucky Lewis had shown up when he did. Sam had been gaining momentum. Sucked to be saved by an old man.

No matter. He didn't owe him shit. Thomas was going to make sure it was the last favour the old fart ever did for anyone.

He felt his way along the wall of the short hallway that he knew led to the stairs. Most of the smoke was coming from the covered porch out back. A quick glance from where he stood showed him he wasn't stopping anything.

The fire was too far gone. If he had a fire truck, maybe, but on his own, they were shit out of luck. They had all better get out of here before the whole place was in flames.

He didn't know when the big propane tanks would blow, but he doubted there was long to wait. He wasn't going to stick around to wait and see.

Thomas was too big to fit out the window. He barely fit out most doors. He would have to go back out the way he came and deal with Lewis. He couldn't avoid it.

Tonight was the night. And he was almost blind from the mix of smoke and blood in his eyes.

When he got to the kitchen, he was thrown off again. At first he didn't even see the bitch Lewis had sent him in here for. She wasn't very big, but he should be able to see her. This truly was the night of surprises.

He wasn't the type of guy that liked surprises. Even when he was a kid, he liked everything planned and neat. His room was never a mess. His toys all had a place. Tonight was not that at all. Everything was upside down. He wished he was at the gym. Weights were easy. Weights were predictable. Weights made sense, they were just weights, that's all. Weights didn't shoot at you or try to set you on fire.

Why didn't he get a job as a personal trainer? They made good money and had no shortage of hot gym bunnies to bang. Doesn't sound like a bad life. Why was this shit job the one he had chosen? After tonight's cleanup he'd be his own boss and be much happier with his career choices.

There she was, crouching by the sink. "Get over here." He grabbed her by the hair.

"Let me fucking go."

She kicked and screamed like a wildcat. She almost

kicked him in the face somehow. He almost let her go, he was so surprised she had that much fight left in her. It had been a long night already.

64: Stone

John tried his best to help. He had shot at least one bad guy before he was hit, and he hoped the girls could make it out alive.

He had fucked this up, he should have swallowed his pride and asked for help. Even if they had said no he should have tried.

He wanted to get up and save the day, but he felt so tired. His body felt like it was made of cold granite. He could see himself standing up tall and strong, and shooting all the bad guys and saving everyone.

He wanted to save Lynda most of all. Her kindness and strong spirit had made him think maybe they could've had a future, even for a little while.

His arm had never been so heavy, he couldn't move it at all. He willed it to move, he even tried to speak to his hand and say, "Move, damn you," but it didn't help. His voice was barely a whisper and his hand didn't listen.

The gun was still in his hand but it was useless now. He saw it all happen in his mind's eye, but his body didn't move an inch and he slowly bled out on the floor of the cabin.

65: In the woods

Lewis was old and tired and, goddamn, tonight he felt every bit of it. Every second of every day weighed on him like a brick. Even killing two women out of the three he shot wasn't enough to make him feel invincible. He should have been on top of the world, and soon he would be, but right at this moment he just felt old and so tired. Once the junkies were all dead, he'd feel better.

"Get back in here, Tom." He coughed a long, ragged cough. The fucking smoke wasn't helping any. Why the fuck couldn't Bobby have waited a little longer? Bobby wasn't as smart as Lew once thought he was.

He leaned on the fake wood panel wall to steady himself, but the gun and the hand holding it never wavered an inch. "Line these fuckers up and kill them. We are so done with these losers."

"Jane is pregnant, please don't hurt her," Sam begged.

"So fuckin' what? It doesn't matter now if it ever did. Jane has to die. You all do. Maybe I'll shoot her first, so you can watch her and your baby die and know it is all your fault. Or I'll shoot you first. We will see what end of the line I start at."

Lewis coughed but couldn't clear his throat. It was like his lungs were jumping right out of his mouth.

When he finally found some breath, he said, "There's nothing anyone can do to save any of you now."

66: Smoky rooms

In all the commotion no one noticed Bobby crawl off to hide his bleeding ass somewhere else. Thomas knew him well enough. Thomas knew where he'd be going: to make something blow up. His "pièce de resistance" was going to happen without a hitch, whether the boss said so or not. The soon-to-be the old boss.

He had set a timer, but fuck that. He was going to blow it now. Bobby was bleeding too much to make it out of here anyway. He was going to take everyone he could with him. Fuck Lewis, fuck Thomas, too, for that matter. They could both suck his hairy nuts in hell.

He always kept a shiny Zippo in his pocket, every day since he was nine. He stole the first one from his old man. It took him a few minutes to pull the lighter out of his pocket since his right arm wasn't working properly any-more. It even slipped out of his fingers not once but twice, because his hand was slick with his own blood. He had had plenty of other people's blood on his hands in his life, but having his own blood all over the place was a first.

He flicked open the lighter and caught a whiff of the fuel. He loved that smell. His whole life. Some people hated it, found they could taste the lighter fluid in whatever they smoked. He usually flipped the lighter around a few times to amuse ladies who were easily im-pressed by fast, shiny things, like his car.

Now he was so fucked up, he had to hold the lighter with both hands to even get a spark. He didn't know how this could have happened to him. He wasn't surprised about Jim's abrupt ending; he hadn't been smart or careful. But Bobby was always careful, he planned the shit out of everything. He was always thorough. Earlier he had set up a backup for the backup. So now all that was left to do was one flick of the Zippo in the right place.

If he had been planning things, tonight would never have happened. He wouldn't have used the same guys twice, and whoever he used would have been way too scared to fuck him over. If only he'd been the boss. He would have killed the two idiot mules right off the bat when they didn't show at the drop. No excuses, no questions. None of this kidnapping, give me back my shit, bullshit.

It was near pitch black in the room, so the tiny spark from the flint was blinding. He dropped the lighter again.

There were still a few minutes left on the timer. No matter. No time to wait. Bobby lit the fuse and watched it burn. It was so pretty. He felt a twinge of regret that he wouldn't be seeing any more fires.

To someone looking in the window, he must have looked like some bloody, maniac child, happily awaiting the end of the world.

67: Timing

Thomas was watching Bobby's every insane move from the doorway. There was so much smoke he wasn't quite sure what he was seeing was real at first.

He pulled the pin on the fire extinguisher he had grabbed from the hallway and covered both Bobby and the device in front of him in fluffy white foam to drench the fuse.

Bobby couldn't have looked more surprised if the Easter bunny had walked through the door. That made Thomas giggle. Despite everything going on around him, he was tickled by blasting someone with a fire extinguisher. He wished he had a video. He felt like a clown fireman; all that was missing was the floppy shoes.

Hr swiped the device off the floor in his big hands and ripped it in two. That clock would never finish its countdown.

"What the fuck are you doing? It's going to blow anyway!" Bobby sputtered.

"I'm just following the boss's orders. He said put it out. For now. Look at this place, nothing can stop it from burning now. We have to get out of here."

"Just leave me. I'm fucking dying anyway."

"Boss said get Bobby, so I'm getting Bobby. Who said you were dying? You ain't a doctor. I'm not leaving you here. I need you with me if I want to take over."

"You still want to?"

"More than ever. This is the night. If it doesn't happen tonight it never will. So come on, you crazy asshole, let's go kill Lew."

The fire was growing larger outside the cabin. Thomas didn't have a big enough fire extinguisher to stop that. The back porch was engulfed. The dry firewood piled up under the porch roof was all burning. Soon the black tar shingles would catch. They were already smoking. You would need an entire fire department to stop it now.

He grabbed Bobby by the bloody collar and dragged him back down the hallway to the living room, where Lew was waiting with the two women and Sam. He would have to work fast to stay ahead of the fire. He wondered if the two big propane tanks would wait long enough.

68: Promotion

Thomas dragged the now-unconscious, still bleeding Bob along behind him.

"What took you so long? This ain't a fuckin' picnic."

"It was hard to see through all the smoke, boss."

"Is he dead?"

"He is still alive for now. Barely."

"All right, if he makes it out of here, we'll get him to my doctor friend. Shoot these three assholes, so we can get out of here."

"Sure, boss."

Thomas took out his gun and pointed it at Sam, then over to Lynda and back to Jane in the middle. They all screamed and tried to huddle closer together. His finger tightened on the trigger as he waved the gun back and forth.

Then he swung the gun toward Lewis and fired. A neat little hole appeared in his chest. Lew couldn't have looked more surprised if Jesus had walked in the door.

Tom had always thought he would have a lot to say to the boss before he offed him, but he didn't have any special speech. He kept it simple. He was too tired for this shit. "Goodbye, old man, I won't miss you at all."

He fired again, and another hole materialized just above Lew's blue eyes.

He watched Lewis fall to the floor and then turned his gun back towards the three hostages. The gun fired again, and this time it was Sam who yelped. The three of them scattered across the room. The girls ran out the door like scared mice. He couldn't see Jane and Lynda, but he would find them as soon as he was done with Sam. He wanted to finish off Sam first.

The little fucker scurried behind the couch, like that offered any real protection. No bulletproof couches here, or anywhere.

Tom grabbed the end of the couch and flung it end for end across the room like it was made of Styrofoam. And there was Sam, a fish not even in a barrel.

69: Time

Sam had stared in disbelief at the holes in Lew's chest and forehead. Then the girls ran.

He was so surprised at not being dead he didn't do anything for a split-second. Lynda pulled Jane out the door into the pouring rain with her. They weren't stopping for anything. He doubted a cement wall would have stopped them.

Thomas was standing there with Bobby bleeding on the floor behind him, slowly bringing up his gun. Sam dove over the couch.

As he landed, his fingers touched the cold steel of Lynda's gun. He knew he wasn't a good shot but this close, he couldn't miss. He had to not miss.

The couch rose up away from him like a leaf in the wind, so no more time to think. He shot Thomas in the chest twice.

In slow motion Tom fell like a big pine tree, landing square on Bobby. If Bob had been alive, he probably wasn't anymore. Thomas weighed more than a ton of bricks.

Sam didn't wait to see if they were all dead or just partly. He went out the screen door after Lynda and Jane.

When his foot hit the bottom step, there was a thunderous boom, and he was flying. It was like a big, warm hand picked him up and threw him hard across the yard. He landed in a tangle of arms and legs beside Bobby's half-dead car.

Lynda and Jane were already getting in Lynda's car at the end of the driveway. He ran toward them, as best he could.

Jane opened the back door, and he jumped in. They sped away while the whole place burned in the early light of dawn.

70: Road home

Lynda drove the little car around all the big puddles and bumps. Jane was curled up in a ball in the passenger seat. John's car was still stuck in the muck.

There was a cop car parked across the road and a police officer shining a flashlight into the ditched car. He waved for her to stop.

She said, "Officer we need your help."

He answered. "What happened to you? We've been looking for you, are you okay?"

"We're okay." She sounded surprised, even to herself.

"You don't look like you are okay. Have you seen Officer Tower tonight?"

"Yes! John was helping us, or he tried to. He was shot last time I saw him, I don't know if he was even alive. The building was on fire. There was a huge explosion. We just got out of there. I am so happy to see you! It's not far from here, please get help. Please help John!"

He was already on his radio. "Officer down, officer down, assistance requested. We need the fire department, ambulances and tow trucks. Bring everyone you can. Injured civilians, maybe an active shooter. I found the missing girl and her sister. We're way out of town on the Jones Road."

"How did you finally find us?" Lynda said when she could get a word in.

"I tracked John's phone and it lead me to this car. And

you."

Lynda turned off the ignition. "Lucky me."

71: Down the road

Chris went to Trisha's place and tore it apart looking for the bag. *What kind of bag?* He should have asked. If he found more than one, he would take them all.

But in the little apartment, he found nothing. She didn't have much stuff to look through, either. It was a very small place.

He checked her car, not the best place to hide anything. He should have checked there first. He found a black garbage bag full of heroin jammed half under her spare tire.

Now what to do with it? He took out his phone and brought the list of callers up showing the last number that called him. His thumb hovered over the call button.

Chris looked at the phone and back at the bag. He decided he didn't want to be a part-time bouncer, part-time dispatcher at a shitty strip club anymore. It was time to move on, this town held nothing for him.

He threw the bag in the trunk of his old beater car and threw the cell phone in the ditch. They'd never find him. By the time they even knew he was gone he would be in another country.

No one in this hick town knew him, anyway. He wouldn't miss this place. It bored him, all there was was ocean and trees. Nice to visit but not to live.

He had always been a drifter, no connections to anyone or anywhere, so he was sure they couldn't find him. Chris wasn't even his real name. It was what came out when Thomas asked him his name. He could have just as easily said Dan, or Mark, or Blaine. He had so many aliases he barely knew who he was anymore.

He was a man of opportunity, and he was going to grab this one with both hands. He knew a place to get rid of this bag of goodies fast, with no questions asked. Then he'd head somewhere warm, maybe Mexico, shave his beard, maybe dye his hair blonde and get a nice crispy tan.

Life was good.

72: New beginnings

Denise stretched in her big, comfy bed and wished she had someone to cuddle with. Then it would really be comfy. Maybe she should ask Sara to move in, then she would have her morning cuddles.

It was time for her to go pick up Mikey; she needed to be closer to her baby. He would be hungry and the fever was long gone. Some breakfast and he'd be all set. He was a fighter; she wasn't surprised. He looked like her, and already he was showing the same strong temperament as his mama. She would call her niece and see if he was awake yet.

When the phone buzzed, she figured it was her morning kisses from sweet Sara. Or her niece saying Michael was up. Ugh. It was just an unknown number. It was no one.

She never answered those calls. It was always a telemarketer or some heavy-breathing stalker from work. She'd had a few of those in her years at the club. She let it go to message. Then it started buzzing again. She turned it off. She wasn't awake enough for stalkers.

Any woman knew what she meant. You didn't have to be a dancer to get harassed, you just had to be a woman. She had gotten plenty of unwanted advances from sleazy people, both in person and the more cowardly ones who called and hung up over and over again. She usually ended up changing her number. Somehow they kept getting it and calling her no matter how many new numbers she got. She had even tried getting Sara to get her a phone under her name, and still it continued.

If she didn't have her Mikey, she would get rid of the phone altogether. She might do that, anyway. Get off the goddamn grid, go live in a cabin by a river somewhere.

Finally, she checked her messages. There were a lot of them. A few were hang-ups, and one heavy breather, but some were very important.

When she truly realized what had happened to her lover, she went into the bathroom to get the bag that was to blame. Pulled it out of the closet, opened it and dug through the towels, finding no heroin.

Denise just sat on the cold tile floor, surrounded by her own dirty laundry, and cried.

73: Jail

Bobby was going to be here for a long, long time. This was the one place he never wanted to be. If he hadn't listened to Lewis, he wouldn't be here.

Sure he was alive, but what life was this? His arms and hands were covered in scars. He would remember that night every time he looked at his hands.

By the time he got out of this hole, he would be an old man, older than Lewis had been. He wouldn't be the boss of anything. He was a low-level criminal who had gotten caught, and he was going to pay the price for all their crimes. Someone had to. The newspapers had to have someone to blame.

Once the cops found out who was who, and who was still alive after the smoke cleared. Bobby was the one who took the fall for everything. Thanks to the wire Sam had worn, there was hard evidence of him committing murder and attempting more. He was the only one left to blame. After all his planning and hard work, he ended up being the jail dummy. He would decide if being alive like this was better or worse than being dead like all the others. There was plenty of time to decide, years and years.

Deep down he knew it wasn't Lewis's fault. Or anyone else's. It had been his own doing. All by his little lonesome. He had brought himself to this place. That was what he had to live with. That was what bothered him, not the murders or any of the other things he had done. It was that he had made every choice that put him here. It was all on him.

He rolled over and faced the ugly, pictureless cell wall. It was exactly the same view as all the other walls in here. Grey and endless. Walls of insanity. Soon he would be insane, if he wasn't already. He was already in solitary "for his own protection."

Other cons had attacked him the first day he arrived in this place. Guards had broken it up before he was dead, but they let it go long enough that he had ended up in the infirmary for a few days.

He didn't even get to go outside. He had lost track of how many days he had been in this tiny room full of stale dead air. It protected him from the inmates.

Working for Lewis, being the muscle, he had made no friends, and a lot of his not-friends were in here. He was a walking target. The new crew taking over wanted to be sure no one from Lewis's old crew was ever coming back to haunt them.

They put the word out there that he was a rat. One thing guys in jail don't like very much is rats. It would make his life interesting.

It was the guards he was more worried about. He was a convicted cop killer. The guards might just kill him themselves. There were a couple he was sure wouldn't lose a wink of sleep over it.

He doubted he would have to take his own life. He would just have to decide how hard he wanted to fight when the time came.

A simmering pot of anger, Bobby couldn't stop himself from punching the wall. He screamed and punched until his knuckles were raw and bleeding through scars. "Fucking junkies!"

At least the blood on the wall changed the view.

74: Rehab

Sam rolled over in the narrow bed and looked out the tiny window at the misty grey skies. The air was soggy, even inside it felt like it was almost ready to rain. It reminded him of that night.

He tried not to think about it. He blamed himself for it all. He couldn't help it. The guilt was killing him.

He thought about Adam and Trisha, John, even that girl Sara from the club. He had only met her once. Not to mention all the dead bad guys. He knew she was really the one to blame, but deep down he'd always believe it was his fault. He should never have been involved with Thomas.

He would have to live with it, or give up and die. If he didn't stay straight and sober, he wouldn't live long. He knew if he started using again he'd use and use until he overdosed. Trying to drown the memories.

He had to focus on Mikey. If he did good here and kept showing he was a good person, he would be able to see him more and more. If he could get and hold a job, stay off the drugs, and booze. Maybe he could be a Dad to Mikey and the new baby, who was due any day now.

They had been through a lot, but Jane was young and strong. The doctors expected the birth to go off without a hitch. He had a healthy daughter on the way; he wanted to be part of her life. Jane hadn't seen or spoken to him yet. He had gotten the info from her sister. A letter, more of a note. All it said was, "Jane and baby to be are fine. We don't live here anymore. Don't contact us."

She hated him, too. He hated himself. They had brought him to the hospital, but then they pretty much cut him off. He didn't blame them one bit, but it still hurt.

He was trying to give them space (he didn't have much choice while he was in here, anyway.) He hoped someday Jane would forgive him and let him be part of the baby's life. He would understand if she didn't, but he would do everything he could to make sure she did.

For now, all he could do was stare at the wall and think about his children, them growing up without him, and all the things he would miss.

75: Fresh start

The little zig-zag lines on the paper were getting bigger, more jagged. The pains were getting stronger and lasting longer. Jane would be in full labour soon. It was real this time, no false labour, the baby was coming.

Jane had been so afraid this day would never come. She squeezed her sister's hand. The good one, not the one that was tied in a sling, the one that had been shot and was wrapped up like a mummy's arm.

"Lynda, it's almost time. I'm so scared! After the kidnapping I thought I would lose the baby. I thought we would both die."

"Shhh, don't worry about that now. Look at this beautiful hospital. Aren't you glad we chose this town to live in? It's so clean and shiny! Both you and the little one inside you are far too strong to be stopped. You can do this, the doctor, and nurses do this all the time. I bet the nurses can do it without the doc even being here. Some women give birth just fine in much worse places than a bright, warm hospital."

"I know it is nice here, and the doctors and nurses are amazing. Not in a hurry at all. It will be okay, just don't leave me alone. Please stay here."

"Wild horses couldn't drag me outta here, and you know it's true, sister!" Lynda kissed Jane square on top of her nose.

Jane knew it was true, Lynda would always do everything she could to take care of her little sis. Lynda was more like a mother than a sister. She had been thrust into the role by a horrible accident, but she had done a good job ever since. Maybe even better than their own mother might have done, Jane hoped Lynda knew how much that meant to her.

She squeezed Lynda's hand and smiled. Soon her sweet little girl would come into this world and meet her mother, and one day possibly her father. When the kid was 18 and went looking. Right now he wasn't going to see any of them. He had to complete his rehab.

She didn't know if she wanted to ever see Sam again, anyway. She would always love him a little but she knew she couldn't trust him. He had lied to her so many times there was no trust left. Even him saving her life hadn't given her faith in him or his promise to be better.

Until she knew that he wasn't the same old Sam any-more, he would not play a very big part in her life. When he proved he loved himself and them more than the things that got him into trouble, she might try to let him in again. Or maybe it would be smarter to just shut him out and move on. Decisions that would have to wait for now.

"You know you do have to deal with Denise," Lynda said. "Not right yet, but soon. This little one has a big brother. It would be wrong to not let siblings know each other."

"I know, but that connects us back to Sam and I don't need that right now. I'll think about it, all of it. That stuff is all I have been thinking about. Just not right now. Now I have to think about meeting my daughter."

Acknowledgements

I'd like to thank the team at Moose House: Andrew Wetmore for his encouragement and editing, Rebekah Wetmore for her amazing cover artwork and Brenda Thompson for being an inspiration and believing in rural Nova Scotia authors.

Angel Flanagan

About the author

Angel Flanagan lives beside Saint Mary's Bay, Nova Scotia with her husband, two sons, and three cats.

Rugged Nova Scotia coastlines with roaring winds and crashing waves inspire her. She enjoys walking the beaches, while hunting for tiny sea glass treasures from the past. She explores a fascination with changing landscape and abandoned places throughout her work. When not writing or taking photos, Angel grows her own vegetables and even has a few chickens.

Flanagan's work has been published in *The Chronicle Herald*, *Le Courrier de la Nouvelle Ecosse*, *Xalt Magazine*, *Coastal Life Magazine*, *The Lobster Bay Shopper* and *The Clare Shopper*. One of her short stories appears in *Moose House Stories Volume 1*.

Flanagan's author website is **angelflanagan.com**.

Lost and Found is her first novel.